The Girl Upstairs

Monica C. Petter

First Published by Monica C. Petter

ISBN: 978-0-578-12195-6

Printed by Instantpublisher.com

Cover Art © Monica C. Petter

II

• • •

Dedication

For David....38,000 words to love by.

June 2010

• • •

Red Dresses

Rory carried herself the same as always. Her frame was tightly manned as if to anchor her every step with purpose against the shifting sands. She moved in the opposite direction and twenty-year-old perfume rushed

Holden as he stood in the Gulf's balmy wind. The scent oddly nauseated and aroused him. Holden had arrived unnoticed, just as Rory embraced her former sister-in-law, Madison, and the small boy that bobbled between them. Three years might not have waned if he had just called Rory when he heard of her brother's death. Madison was a striking woman. Rhett had liked all the women in his life to be beautifully controlled. Although their distance was roughly one hundred and fifty feet, Madison caught Holden studying the two of them. He stepped out of Madison's view.

From behind, Rory's red sleeveless sundress flaunted ... her strong shoulders as she talked with her hands. Even when she was a child, they were always connected by invisible strings to her wide, articulate mouth. Sound bites of her words and laughter boomed over the roar of the high tide. Madison handed Rory a large manila envelope. The women shared a final

embrace. Rory's low whispers bounced on the wind, her inflection loving. Holden remembered that soft southern nuance echoing off the walls of their bedroom. Rory turned around, seeing Holden sitting on the steps. Her green eyes downturned to the sand as she cradled the envelope under one arm like a football. She puckered her lips in concentration and began that purposeful saunter, holding the dress up to her knees with the other hand. Dresses had always made Rory insecure.

Holden stood, finishing a beer as his tragic past walked toward him. He threw his empty bottle at Rory's feet. She dropped the envelope

● ● ●

in the sand. They studied each other, toes to brow, before both reflexively bent down to pick up the envelope, bumping shoulders, their lips and noses invading personal boundaries. The scent of her hair and skin rushed him, betraying his logic. The energy was chemical. Holden picked up the envelope, grabbing Rory as she bobbled, letting his firm hold on her forearm linger.

She chewed her lower lip.

"Dresses…they make me crazy." Rory plumbed his soul with her green stare.

"Red has always been your color." He caressed her fingers as he slid the envelope into her hand. Rory dusted sand off the envelope over and over.

They looked up at the beach house's weathered exterior. Gabrielle's parents had always invited them to summer vacations the last ten years of Gabby's life. The chipping paint

● ● ●

revealed the many layers and varied colors applied over the years. The air was foreign without the Vansants.

"What's in the envelope?" Holden watched Rory deliberate the seal.

"Gabby's journals." Rory tossed them glibly onto the patio. She hiked up her dress, falling onto the top step clumsily. She was rigid, distant.

Holden eased beside her. He could feel her energy again. It was red hot, angry and full of shame he couldn't begin to comprehend. High tide drowned them in white noise. There were no words necessary as they sat idle, deliberating whether to cross back over the line in the sand. He had his own anger that consumed him in wild, unpredictable fits. Misplaced and misunderstood, masking his sadness.

• • •

The chrome from a sailboat blinked out a Morris code as they remembered another lifetime's mast and sail. Holden offered his hand to Rory, his palm facing the indigo sky. Rory traced his faint lifeline with her index finger. His life had been erased with Gabby's death.

* * *

June 1990

• • •

6

• • •

A Vansant Beach House Summer

Holden and Rory walked the beach hand in hand after sneaking out of the beach house as the Vansants slept. The crescent moon lent light and shadow for the dark walk to the marina. John Vansant was an oddly private man respectfully feared as they were growing up. His boat was docked bayside at the marina near Ft. Morgan. He had always kept it away from the other boats, secluded. Their silhouettes fell off the dock and into the boat with the precision of thieves. Holden closed the cabin door with one hand as he slid his other hand around Rory's supple hips. Everything old and lasting in their childhood friendship seemed exotic and new as they dabbled in love. Holden wasn't fast or furious with Rory. He understood how she thought. Her green eyes were jade lanterns to her heart. Their kisses were audible, their novice poetry. Their words were in the tips of their fingers. Fingers that unfastened

* * *

buttons and walked the spine. Holden popped the clasp and her lacy red bra fell onto the moonlit floor. He buried his face deep in her cleavage, kissing tenderly the warm skin that clouded his reasoning, forcing them to keep their relationship covert. Holden knew Rory's older brother had a conditioned control over her and Gabrielle. He had watched the power Rhett exercised when they were all growing up together in their neighborhood.

Rory had been guiding Holden's gentle kisses with his ears that she suddenly gripped in fear as a quick, black outline moved past the cabin window. They heard a small thump followed by familiar voices, vibrations of scurried movement through the boat. Their labored breathing quieted, as they concentrated on the verbal fight ensuing outside. Rory recognized the shrieks as Gabby's. Out of her periphery, Rory saw Gabby on the starboard side, flailing wildly before splashing into the bay. Then, thunderous steps

* * *

rocked the port side of the boat, and the shadow fixed his crazed pallor on Rory. Holden chased after the dark ghost, interrupting their intimacy. Rory was searching out the window for Gabby when John Vansant grabbed her head, thrashing it against the wall. She frantically swung at the gray air. Holden shattered the opened window with his fist, showering glass that broke John's grip. John raced out the door, forever a slave to the daylight.

Holden held Rory tightly to his chest. He covered her nakedness with his shirt. Adrenalin flushed his cheeks. The dead end road at Fort Morgan was untraveled at midnight, but he was conflicted, something deep inside didn't want to leave Rory alone. Her head was bleeding and she was semi-conscious. He knew he needed to search for a phone and call for help. Rory's breathing changed to an odd rhythm. Then, he remembered a payphone at the gas station adjacent to the marina.

● ● ●

"I'm going for help…I love you." Holden gently kissed Rory's forehead. She groaned softly in acceptance.

Later, Holden fixated on Rory's innocent face as she was prepared for the ambulance. He could still taste her clean perfume on his lips. The police found some of Gabby's personal effects in the water along with blood on the side of the boat. Time stood still as their lives were spiraling apart. Lexie Vansant had arrived with the police. She coddled the twenty-three-year-old children she had always called her own, comforting with her stoic and strong facade. Her pupils weren't yet prepared for the grief and tragedy that had just been sewn.

* * *

April 2010

Between The Miles

What do you say to two people whose lives you ruined? How do you apologize, rationalize justice over love? Do you just wait for the swift slap to the face? The cold "I hate you" in their pain? Is there any good in all the lies, deception, and evil in the world? I wonder every waking moment. I have for the past twenty years. I have analyzed this tragedy and tried my hardest to find a way things could have curved to the left or to the right, but it seemed like everything happened so quickly. There was no time to think it through. I had to act on each grenade as it was thrown to me, disengaging it with more pain, more lies. I have gotten good at deception. I am not proud of it. It may have taken twenty years, but I am rectifying the pain I have inflicted out of my own fears.

Will folded Lexie Vansant's letter back into its well-worked creases. He kept going back to that particularly intense portion of the letter.

* * *

It had him traveling to Seattle, moved by his parents' past he desperately needed to comprehend. Will had always known his mother and uncle harbored secrets surrounding his absent father. But, Rhett was dead and couldn't strong arm them with protection any longer. He sat in the drive at Mrs. Vansant's cabin marveling the majesty in the quaint wooded scenery, not fathoming his own manic grip on the steering wheel. He put the car in park and turned the key, shutting the engine off. The roar of nature was a battle cry from something larger than he.

Lexie's small cabin was on an isolated hillside, hiding her from the terrors and regrets of her life. She had gotten lost in the soothing sounds of nothingness high up in dizzying altitudes. Cancer was claiming her. She was home with hospice care. Her nurse had washed her hair and dressed her presentably. No makeup could hide death's slow signature, but she at

● ● ●

least wanted to resemble some semblance of the woman that had loved Will's parents. She knew this meeting with him was delicate but pivotal.

There were fresh flowers from the forest on the small kitchen table and she lay on the special bed bought for her constant pain, furniture now torture to her body. She admired old photos of Rory and Holden in their childhood and adolescent years. They anchored the tables throughout the small space.

Will moved through the doorway, his eyes chasing the wall lined with odd-sized photos of Gabby from birth to death. In between was framed poetry that broke up the images with words and symmetry, lending the walls voice. The beeping monitors were the only sounds. Lexie stared out the window, lost in her own thoughts, thick as smoke floating in the air. Her face was ashen, her eyes black pools, sunken and dark. Her hair was white, short and spiked, yet

● ● ●

she was alluring at sixty-five. Will was a handsome combination of Rory and Holden.

"I'm Will Peacock." Will extended his hand to her. She clasped his tender, young fingers tearfully.

"Yes, you are." She patted his hand as she looked out the window. It had rained that morning and she watched the few remaining dew drops race down the glass, finally reaching the sill.

"I got your letter. I don't know what I'm doing here…" he lied to himself. He wasn't emotionally savvy, just a baby taking his first steps, unprepared for the hard falls.

"Yes, you do, William Holden. Own it."

"I don't have anything to own." He sighed in frustration.

Will studied a picture of Lexie embracing his mother and father, as Gabby sat at her mother's feet front . . . and center. It was placed on the night stand beside her bed, partially hidden by tissues and medication bottles.

Lexie motioned to a chrome dining chair with a red shiny seat cushion that sat oddly alone in the corner. He pulled it close to her bedside so he could hear her shallow voice.

"I know your uncle, Rhett, kept your parents apart. He was a pompous bastard even as a child. But, he loved you and your mother." Her honesty was gentle despite the harsh, uneven tones in her words.

"He never liked my father." Will's green eyes mirrored his mother's hot passion. The bitterness ebbed as he mumbled.

"Rhett protected you all and that was the point... That's a long root you'll never unearth."

"Protected us from what? Why should I help you? Your husband killed your daughter and almost killed my mother." He thrust the chair back into the corner. Lexie envied his courage.

● ● ●

"You have everyone else's reasons to walk away and let this die and let me die with it. It is *your* questions, *your* reasons that brought you here."

Will regretted his accusations instantly. They weren't his sentences, but others he had fed upon.

"My mother has that same photo."

Will reached for her frail hand, letting the photo disarm his anger and disappointment, pushing hope back to the surface.

"Your parents need to know what really happened the night my Gabby died. You are my answer." Lexie's black eyes shimmered, a beacon to her pain.

"What do you want me to do?" Will's expression screamed of innocence anticipating fate.

"Rhett kept Gabby's journals when she died. Contact your aunt, Madison Peacock.

Find those journals. When I'm gone, they'll explain everything that I won't...that I can't." Regret lowered her last syllable to a whisper. His eyes left hers, gravitating back to the picture of his parents.

The Call

Lexie now had Will's trust and cooperation, an impressionable shard of a young man's virtue in her pocket. She would handle this rib off the same DNA with a learned respect she hadn't understood the first time. Lexie had set wheels in motion and inertia would finish the job whether she was alive or not.

Lexie stared at the photo. John was unrecognizable, his hair long and matted, his face covered in a wiry silver beard. Lexie tilted the photo sideway, looking into John's

* * *

wide opened brown eyes. Eyes filled with mania from bargaining with terrorists. It was the only physical feature that revealed small traces of the man he had once been.   The gunshot wound to John's temple had finally silenced his psychosis. She could tell John had struggled. His hands were bruised, bathed in blood. Attached to the photo was the research John had constructed all the years of estrangement, the key to their plight.

Her bony fingers dialed the number she had memorized backwards in her head. It had been months since they had spoken last. There was no telling what time zone she was in. She bounced around, a gypsy without a history. The rings felt eternal. They mocked her urgency.

She was groggy, asleep when she answered. Lexie's voice seized just hearing the sound of her voice.

• • •

"My Gabrielle, it's over. You are safe. Come to me. You know you have to finish what you started."

The redwood birds chirped their ode to spring while Gabrielle sobbed a long, inconsolable symphony of relief.

● ● ●

May 2010

. . .

• • •

The Letter

My dearest Rory and Holden,

If you are reading this, I have died. John is finally dead. So much time has passed that there seems little justice in that now. I suppose we are left to find the lessons in the rampages on our sanity. Rhett helped me protect us all the only way I knew how at the time, by keeping us apart. John came too close to you both many times over the years. Fear was the only way I had learned to live and my only regret would be instilling that sense of anxiety in you. I don't regret my actions. I have reconciled my past and know what I sacrificed because of John will be paid forward to you if there is any such thing as karma.

Please, I want you to put an end to the past, make peace, and be honest with yourselves — regardless of the outcome. Own your part or it will own you.

* * *

I am leaving you both the beach house.
Go there. My lawyer will be in touch.

All my love, Lexie

Rory Peacock

Rory walked into her Philadelphia condo after locking the metal lid to her mailbox. She glanced back over her shoulder, cutting her hazel eyes to dark corners for shadows. It was a simple action she had done for twenty years in this small space once Rhett's. She had made it livable for Will, but it would never be her home. She heard William systematically opening drawers, searching quietly for something. Rory had memorized his sounds down to his breathing. Their every move seemed monitored in protection from the outside world. Will acknowledged her entrance with a smile that held Holden's charm. Will was a good man,

● ● ●

forced to grow up early. Rory had never lied to her son, cautiously telling him what he needed to know. Their way of living was established as his norm.

Since Rhett's death, Rory noticed Will acting out his anger and restlessness. The television was a low roar as a weatherwoman spoke energetically of spring showers.

Rory placed the mail on the weathered mahogany table where a land line phone had once sat. Rory had called Holden infrequently after the tragedy because Rhett had caught her talking to him and cut off all calls, paying Holden a stern visit. John seemed to be everywhere, leaking into the wallpaper and through the wiring. When Rory's pregnancy test was positive, she hid her growing belly, fearing John would slither up into her womb, taking yet another joy.

Rory thumbed through the bills and credit card advertising when she recognized Lexie's distinctive cursive ... handwriting. The envelope seemed to breathe, speaking to her in a southern, Arkansas accent. She unfolded the linen paper. Lexie was dead. Someone who had once been so close to her, part of her very fiber was gone, and Rory couldn't feel anything.

Apparently, Lexie had instructed someone to scrutinize Rory's outgoing mail as a precaution. Inside the large envelope was a letter Rory had sent to Holden in 2007 after Rhett's death. It still had a fresh stamp on it, ready to mail. On the outside of the envelope Lexie had written *Forgive me, Rory. It wasn't safe to send.* Rory held the letters side by side – Lexie's in her left hand and Holden's in her right. Anger was starting to pull Rory under, threatening to drown her in sorrow. Her hands began to shake, her lips quivered uncontrollably. Tears pooled in the corners of her clear, green eyes. She dropped the letters, sliding to the floor. Will moved around the corner, picking up the letters as his mother bellowed her resentment off the high ceilings. The irony was

● ● ●

stripping all her walls, allowing the vulnerable young woman of twentythree she had once been to show her true face.

Will read Lexie's letter, then the letter his mother had written to Holden.   His morbid curiosity was like witnessing a car crash, difficult to process. The carnage had been strewn into odd poses. The eyes focused, but the brain was numb. The realization that they were finally free was now bittersweet. Will knelt down, putting his arms around his mother as Rory wept into her hands. Betrayal was forging a new path.

"Maybe it's not too late?" Will sounded six years old bursting with forgotten hope for a father he had never known.

The Stolen Letter

August 2007

● ● ●

Holden,

I remember how your hands felt. They were rough and calloused around the fingertips, but there was gentleness in the way they maneuvered everything they touched. I knew your footsteps as they approached, memorized the way your shoes hit the pavement as you walked. Your eyes were kind in their crystal design. Because we grew up together, we became more than best friends rather easily. You knew me to the core and that was what had allured and scared me. I was in love with you when Gabby died. But, I ran away from us. Only now do I realize I will always be in love with you.

I was lost until I found out I was pregnant with our son. William Holden saved my life. I didn't trust my feelings back then. I should have trusted in you. I had already lost you, wasn't strong enough to reach back or tell you about Will.

• • •

Our life without you has been shallow. But, Rhett has just recently died and his paranoia has left me haunted by my fear and shame. I lied to myself, saying I was too afraid of my brother. Now that he's gone, I see keeping Will from you has been selfish. After I had to cut all contact with you, I died in places that belonged to us. Will was my way of keeping the only bits of you for me. I want you to know your son. Someday, William needs to know you. Things still aren't safe until John is found. I just want to give you the knowledge that has always been rightfully yours.

Always ~Rory

Holden Hitchfield

The bar was packed for NASCAR. The races were popular even in the nestled hills of Breckenridge. Now Gabby's housed only the faithful   regulars. ● ● ●   The   announcers had their own bets as to who would win and usually changed their minds in a split second. Holden watched his "rat pack" of sorts chastise and cheer. The larger than life commentators on the new big screen Holden had recently purchased, coupled with the unusual heat, made the newest nightly special *The Ruby Slipper* more enticing. It was a refreshing combination of vodka, tonic, and cranberry.

A writer friend of Holden's came up with the catchy name after sharing more with him than her flowery vocabulary. She told him she had liked "the way the crimson dotted the table tops and found the reflective qualities of the ice impressive." He didn't really care how she said it. He loved hearing her southern accent. It reminded him of his childhood in Little Rock. The camaraderie could have been mistaken as Holden's family reunion of aunts, uncles and cousins. Yet, Holden had no siblings and his mother had died when he was very young.

● ● ●

Family was a native concept. His family consisted of these men and women who frequently shared their lives over their evening cocktails. They were complex, yet safe.

He mixed a scotch and raised the glass to his tipsy kin. Holden's bartender handed him the mail before Holden retired to his apartment above the bar. His apartment was simple and sparse, rather quiet even with the roar of the crowd down below. He flipped through the usual bills and junk mail solicitations as he swished the sip of scotch around his tongue. He choked, swallowing hard when he caught a glimpse of the familiar curly lines addressing him. The manila envelope grew muscle, almost wrapping around his ribcage and laboring his breathing. He fell back into his recliner. Lexie Vansant had died. Lexie - the one woman he considered his mother. She sacrificed more than most mothers would. In the privacy of that moment, Holden wiped

● ● ●

frustrated tears for this woman who had been difficult to love because of her misunderstood motives. He threw the letter into the stack of junk mail.

The rowdy crowd chimed up again. He reached into his wallet and pulled out a faded photo of Rory. As the roar below turned to chatter, Holden propped Rory's picture against the lamp on the table and questioned her face. As he studied Rory's eyes, he tried to picture them now, speculated they were even more persuasive. This picture of Rory often rebuffed his reason. Rory was looking through him, had always been able to move through him beyond words. It was how they communicated since her brother had always been a controlling asshole in her life. He had strong-armed them with fears of their safety, making his points regarding Gabby's death. Lexie had lived in Seattle, he in Colorado, and Rory in Pennsylvania. Holden had kept his distance

• • •

from them all as promised. Yet, Holden knew Rhett always had an agenda to further in spite of his protection. John was dead and now Lexie was reasoning the twenty years of distance from Rory inconsequential? All Holden could remember about Rory now was the sheer terror on her face the last time he saw her.

Holden dozed off to a montage of sounds, colors, and snippets. His unconscious was forcing him to rediscover deep-seeded feelings he had buried. He couldn't make out Rory's face, but could hear her sexy giggle. Flashes of pink and red roved his unconscious vision. The rhythm of glasses being stacked in the bar below tangled with the dream rhythm of their sexual syncopation. He woke up and groaned in annoyance, rubbing his eyes. The scotch flushed his neck. He rolled over and punched his pillow, staring out the window at the starry midnight. He wondered if the beach home in Alabama haunted Rory with similar

● ● ●

nightmares. A wave of anger burned his stomach and he fumbled for
Lexie's letter on the nightstand. Written at the bottom of the page was Rory's phone number and address.

Chasing Pirates

Rory hung up the phone and stood examining her face in the mirror. Their conversation had been platonic and brief, loaded with booby traps and landmines. What would Holden see when he looked at her now? She wondered if the fine lines around her eyes would give glints of her guilt. She had lied for so long, she couldn't define the truth. A strangely different thought struck like an attack from behind. Had she really *felt* what she was about to do? Had she let herself touch more than the top layer of ... this tragedy?

She gravitated to the safe in her closet and retrieved a metal box containing some old photos and keepsakes. The lid was dusty, shoved into the furthest corner. Rory got a chill up her spine that made her queasy. She pulled at the stiff hinges and found a small envelope with pictures of Will as a baby and various other milestone stages in his life. Precious pictures, private ones she had stowed away just for Holden's eyes - someday - that was now weeks away. Echoes and images invaded her mind as whispers from the past swept over her like shards of broken glass, opening wounds to forsaken anger and remorse. There was a group of photos Gabby had given Rory of their vacations each summer. She flipped nostalgically through their soft, grainy technology. They were so young. Could Rory remember being that young and that carefree?

The red ring box's satin finish tickled her fingertips. It reminded Rory of Holden's

* * *

thoughtful charm. It contained a unique silver ring with three tiny ruby stones. Holden had given it to her after one of the many midnight dates on the boat that last summer. She slid the band on her left ring finger and covered her eyes with the other, praying blindness. For, love and sex had once equaled death. Her body was rejecting the numbing, dull pain she had learned to tolerate. Crystal clear love blindsided her.

* * *

June & July 2010

The Beach House

Holden had memorized Rory walking toward him in her candy-striped bikini. Her hips twisted, bouncing her breasts up and down. He had watched a lifetime of sunsets shimmer and fall through the shadow of her wavy hair. Now, she was off in the distance, running away from him again, her posture and sway was unmistakable, her red dress out of context. Holden opened another beer on the patio. The sun was setting and he leaned over the railing, looking out to the sea. The sky was purple, yellow, and burnt orange, a breathtakingly beautiful evening until Rory had traced the nonexistent lifeline on his palm. Gabby's journals stuffed in the large envelope was their first albatross. A long silence precipitated a deep scrutiny. The magnitude in what they were doing had been overwhelming. This was actual, real, not photos or memories. Rory pulled up the hem of her dress and ran far

● ● ●

down the beach, away from him - again. Holden stared at the envelope Rory had thrown aside. He stomped it, kicking it into the sand.

He slammed the creaky screen as he walked into the empty house with his duffle bag and beer. The house wasn't too large, but maximized its space with an open great room and five bedrooms encircling it. It was weathered and its architecture dated against the backdrop of newer structures now on the beach. The musty smells invaded his senses, provoking memories of summers past. He looked to the narrow stairs, rickety and now warranting

Gabby's "keep out" sign. The upstairs room had served as Gabby's loft, her castle turret. He could almost hear Gabby and Rory chattering as they opened windows to air out the staleness. He tried to remember where the furniture had been. The walls were soft ocean blues and greens and the nail holes highlighted their lonely nakedness.

● ● ●

He polished off his beer and found his old room. Lexie had long taken all the furniture except his and Rory's. He dropped his luggage, staring at the unmade bed. The Vansants always insisted the kids make their beds when they arrived and he noticed Rory had already made hers. He went into the bathroom where the blue seashell border still lined the middle of the room, very 1980's. Instinctively, he opened the cabinet to fetch clean sheets. He grinned at the fresh set folded neatly awaiting him.

Wine and groceries sat on the empty counter. Rory had arrived before him. There was no good light without lamps and the great room was empty. There were some tall, standing candles on the bar meant for softer illumination. Rory had spread a blanket, had prepared a picnic of wheat crackers, cheese, and Vienna sausages.

"Hey..." Rory stood behind him, her red dress sandy, and her eyes red from tears. She was a hot mess.

* * *

"Hey, you… ." He studied the green eyes that contradicted her body language. He was unable to stop blatantly staring at her.

"I'm sorry." She balled her fists, dueling with her self-control.

Holden grabbed the back of Rory's neck and kissed her sniveling lips. She ran her hands through his hair, her needs tactile. She reciprocated fully, whining at times, groaning at others. Then, Rory pulled away from his sincerity, tugging at the constrictions of the hem and neck of her dress. She wiped the wet kisses from the corners of her mouth before nervously tidying his hair she had disheveled. Holden questioned her jade eyes. He had once been a professional at loosening their pregnant pauses. He grabbed her wrist and unzipped the dress that fought to control her body. She gasped for air. He slid the dress off her pink shoulders and she wept in fear.

● ● ●

Their heavy breaths echoed off the emptiness. The phantoms from their past would be the only souls to bear witness. They fumbled to the blanket Rory had prepared. Holden breathed out, Rory breathed in. He noticed the ruby ring he had given her twenty years ago dangling between her cleavage on a silver chain. She stroked the gray most prominent around his temples before diving into his mouth again. Her hands disappeared below his belt line. Holden laced his fingers purposefully in hers, locking their grip before tearing through the sensibility that they had built around them.

Rory's red dress now lay in the middle of the empty room. It screamed brazenly at the cool pastel walls. Their lust had had few real words, just the timely lingo of lovers. Rory was a writer. Holden had never fully conquered the magma in her head. She had felt safest inside herself and that had always made him push as she pulled. Holden watched Rory's shadow move quietly to

* * *

the window. It was dusk and her outline was soft and sensual, yet there was grief in her posture. Her body had ripened nicely with maturity. He wanted more of her, but she disconnected after their sex, reticent.

Rory sighed, walking outside onto the patio, nude as the night. She returned with the envelope he had pummeled into the sand earlier. She threw it on her red dress as he lit the candles she had staged. Rory put on Holden's pull over polo shirt as he buttoned his shorts. For an instant, it was 1990. He opened the bottle of wine she had brought. The wine smelled expensive, subtle, and familiar. It was the same wine they had stolen from the Vansants liquor cabinet twenty plus years ago.

"Do you remember that wine?" Rory watched Holden sip it slowly, his eyes grinning over the glass.

"This used to taste like gasoline. All the best wines do . . . according to teenagers." Holden handed her a glass and reached for the food they had shunned.

"We thought we were so cool." Rory raised her eyebrows. He offered her a bite, but she declined.

"Maybe you did. I just wanted to get you drunk." Holden coveted her braless breasts as she laughed at his blatant honesty.

"Ah, now we know why you own a bar." The fine lines around her eyes rooted their nostalgia.

"I've missed having you...keep drinking." She summoned Holden with a wink to pour a bit more wine.

"We've got a lot of demons. There's not enough sex or alcohol to sate this, you know." Rory frowned skeptically at Holden.

"I'd love to die trying..." Holden reached out for the ring she was wearing around her neck. It was tucked into his ... shirt and he traced the visible outline with his fingers. "…and who says 'sate.' Only a writer."

"This was all I could afford. I practically begged the guy for a deal." Rory watched his fingers crawl up her breast bone, delicate as spider legs, fishing for the chain to the ring. He rolled it between his fingers along with his privy memories of purchasing it.

"When do we broach all those demons?" Rory massaged his graying temples.

"I thought we were trying alcohol and sex first?" Holden flashed a nervous grin. Just reacquainting himself with the spell she cast over him was confusing.

"I can't believe you are really here." Rory moved her hands over his stubbly cheeks, her self-soothing signature.

"This is where we should have been all along." Holden's voice fell in regret, lost in "what if".

● ● ●

"But we're here now...." Rory took the wine glass from Holden's hand and tossed it toward her red dress.

Light of Day

The light of a new day beamed down on Rory through a myriad of windows in the great room. Holden was fast asleep. There was a coffeemaker and a strange array of things left behind while the fundamentals had gone missing. Rory had brought coffee. The aroma roused Holden from slumber.

"A bed...we need a bed." Expletives followed, grumbled from a much older-sounding man than the night before.

"According to my body, it definitely isn't 1990." Rory's back had seized, too, after sleeping on the stone floor. She searched futilely for a spoon. ● ● ●

"This place is a hodge-podge of extras vs. necessities." She poured them both a cup of coffee in paper cups she had found shoved in a back drawer.

"Considering the source, I wouldn't be surprised if Lexie did it on purpose." There was slight contempt in Holden's quip reply.

"Lexie never spoke much about anything - especially surrounding Gabby's death. Rhett said she had good reasons." Rory brushed her hair out of her face as she sipped from her paper cup. "According to Rhett, she had odd sensibilities."

"*According to Rhett* – you always put too much faith in *his* opinions." Holden's lips contorted in mockery of her dead brother.

"God, I forgot what a jackass you are in the morning." Rory turned her back to him. Gabby's journals seemed to have grown legs

• • •

and walked closer to them. The pages' mere proximity swirled a subtle vortex of anxiety.

"I'm tired of talking about dead people. I just don't know how digging up bones has a damn thing to do with us now." Holden kissed the back of her neck apologetically. He dialed his anger down, realizing his terseness when speaking of the dead.

"When do we go upstairs?" Rory blew on her hot coffee, her reticence resurfacing. Holden knew there was loads of misplaced resentment bouncing off the old walls. The pit of his stomach began to sting.

Wet Dreams

Rory and Holden had sidestepped a lot of issues, each feeling the other out, testing the waters of trust. They ... both had secrets they hadn't shared. They both had reasons for their reasons. The morning was humid and thick, ripe with precipitation. The clouds served as a shield, hid their denial nicely. The girl upstairs had almost been averted until the sun began to poke holes in the clouds. Rory swore she smelled Gabby's coconut suntan lotion, Holden heard her calling him with flippant slang. It was as if their very childhood memories were tossing old verbiage at them.

They were getting dressed, showering in a bathroom they had used a thousand times as sandy children sunburned from the beach. The bathroom was now small and cold. Rory tied her robe, drying her hair with a towel. Holden stuck his head in the bathroom doorway, seduced by the smell of her clean skin. She threw her towel at him like a football, knocking his head into the door. She raised her arms in victory, her projectile bull's eye. Holden picked up the towel and

• • •

popped her on the ass. She shrieked, trying to run, but he had a firm grip on her robe collar.

"I used to fantasize about this as a teenager. I always loved how you smelled after a bath. That is why I always let you go first." He put his nose in her hair and closed his eyes. Her shampoo had a hint of rose in it.

"That sounds like *lust*." Rory wilted as Holden put his arm around her waist. He was tall, commanding, using his obstinacy to his advantage.

"Whatever, then I lust you." Holden pinned her against the counter. "We'll start here…on the sink."

"You fantasized about 'doing me' in every room?" Rory laughed as he squeezed her hand with soft duress. It actually could be 1990 for as long as they needed it to be.

• • •

**The tattered poem was taped to the door of Gabby's room.
The paper yellowed and the typing faded.**

The Girl Upstairs
She is the girl
In the attic
That is so misunderstood

She haunts,
She robs you
Of the good

He is a quiet man
He hides-
His poetry undercover

His eyes tell,
Glistening dark pools
Lost for a lover

She's a frightened child
A stoic face,
A well built blank page.

Lost
By circumstance's lot
Frozen at a young age

She's the little girl
Sensitive behind a smile
Older than her years

Imagining lives Juggling
words
Building what she hears.

Everyone has a secret.
There's more buried
Behind the shell

● ● ●

Some lifetimes
Subtly reveal
Their bits of heaven or hell

Everyone has a story.

The Girl Upstairs

It was eerie to read, relatable now. Holden took the key to this sequestered space and wrestled with the frozen lock. When he finally turned it over, he paused, sighing deeply. Rory seemed puzzled, stoic.

The door creaked open and the golden light shone in on an untouched space. The room flashed them back into the early eighties, reminiscent of the Gabrielle they had loved. There were a lot of silent stares and smiles as if walking through a museum of someone famous. It was a time machine, a collector's treasure trove. It even smelled the same, like a cedar closet. Everything seemed so small now, once having such ... weight, gravity, and grandeur. The two of them just stood marveling in the room as it washed them with personal recollections.

Rory walked over to the corner and found the mannequin Gabby used when fathoming the outfit she was going to wear that day. It had her straw cowboy hat and long red wig on its head. The red was now chestnut with dust. On the floor were her white high-top Reeboks whose rainbow laces were braided with the untied fashion statement of the decade. Her easy chair cradled her guitar. Its brown case sat nearby, still hosting colorful stickers all over it. A tape player rested on the brown, aging case with the microphone. Gabby had used it to record her life story on tapes she claimed were hidden under some wooden floor board. On her desk were photos, books, and notebooks of the poems she wrote or the snips of potential ones she would have penned. The walls were papered in her large canvas abstract

• • •

paintings featuring every color of the rainbow. Gabby was a true artist.

Rory squealed as Holden closed the door to the room to find Tom Cruise staring over his Ray Ban's from the movie *Risky Business*. The poster still hung perfectly on the door. Gabby had most likely glued it, the edges sealed tightly while tiny tears dotted the inner frame. She had even threatened to disown her father when he requested she remove the poster in order to paint the chipping door.

"Gabby loved that damn poster." Holden ran his fingers over Gabby's glue work.

"Tom was so hot. What teenage girl didn't own that poster?" They were all so innocent and pure once. Rory put her hands over her mouth, laughing as tears rolled down her fingers.

"My bar family would really understand the place's   meaning ● ● ● with some of these wigs and hats on mannequins…" Holden beat a thick swath of dust off the wig, revealing its glittery red shimmer. "…and that painting, poster and tape player…."

"I'd like to take some of these things back with me if it is alright with you? I know this artist…she'd know exactly where to place these." Rory ran her fingers across an old picture of the three of them. They were no more than ten. Holden watched Rory hold her breath, her hands curling to fists as she placed the photo back on the dusty desk.

"Sounds like you've got a good life back in Breckenridge. You've moved on…nicely." Rory remembered her secret stash of pictures at home, containing this one of the three of them and all the photos of William.

"We all moved forward…right?" Holden reached for Rory's arm, turning her guilty tears

● ● ●

to his eyes. Tears rained down Rory's fingers that now hid her snotty sobs.

1990 began to fade to black as the chirpy ring of Rory's cell phone ushered them into the present. Their baby smooth faces melted into the finely chiseled lines of experience.
She broke from Holden's questioning and bolted down the unsound stairs to her phone.

"I'm sorry I haven't called, dear…no, *no he doesn't know…*" In Rory's hushed haste to get to privacy, she noticed Holden standing in the doorway upstairs. Beams of heavenly light silhouetted him as he listened to her speaking sincerely. As she darted toward the patio, she flashed slight shame in her quick, tepid glint that he almost discounted as guile.

● ● ●

Secrets, Secrets

Rory unwrapped Gabby's journals from the refuted red dress as she slid her cell phone back into her duffle bag. She returned to Gabby's room and the unspoken stifled. Holden stared out the large window, his eyes solemn.

"Let's start with the obvious, what do you say? You are seeing someone and this is now officially complicated." Holden put his hand to his chin, rubbing his whiskers, his lower lip pouting.

"What did you hear to make you think that?" Rory found her secrets heavier with each passing day.

● ● ●

"Did you just come here to go back in time, not forward?" Holden had begun to question Rory's reserve.

"It's not like that. I'm not seeing anyone. There is someone in my life, but we are not romantically   involved."   The
    air   was becoming stagnant and suffocating.

"Christ, Rory! Is that supposed to make me feel better?" He sulked, his pupils firm and steely.

"Do you want to stop? I'm not doing this alone." Rory flung the journals at him, crossing her arms peevishly.

"I don't know what I want to do. I thought I knew…." Holden sat in the window seat, angered and deflated. "I know I don't want to share you with anyone."

● ● ●

"Ah ha - Don't you see the problem? We don't really know each other – *now* – today." Rory sat her ample hips on Holden's lap, pacifying him with flesh, recalling his very fickle pride.

"I know the real you, not this woman you hide behind." Holden ran his hand up her neck, pulling her hair in frustration at this crafty imposter.

"Maybe you do, maybe you don't." Rory kissed him, nursing his puffy lower lip in between her own. She picked up the red journals, handing one to Holden.

"Start reading."

Gabrielle Vansant's Journal

January 1987

● ● ●

Like everyone, I keep a secret from the world. Only a few weeks ago, I was diagnosed with Multiple Sclerosis. MS is an incurable disease with its origins unknown. It is a disaster that affects the central nervous system breaking down the myelin that surrounds the nerves causing strange symptoms. There is currently no treatment other than symptom management. My first symptom can be traced back to 1983 when I was sixteen. I had serious numbness on my right side that eventually moved to the left side.

Strange things happened for years that I didn't understand until now. It took four years, but I feel lucky to know. It finally took a blind spot in on eye to get a diagnosis. Actually, my optometrist caught it and recommended I talk to my father, a neurologist. My parents are wrecks. I have to keep it together especially for my father. He is already talking research and that scares me. I write this so calculated and emotionless like a

* * *

doctor taking dictation, sort of disconnected. It is
because I am trying to process my next moves.

May 1987

Well, it has been three month and lot has
happened. I have been in remission now and have
been gaining my energy back from a bout of
fatigue. School is out so that is an added bonus
since stress seems to worsen my symptoms. I feel
mentally and physically healthier coping now, as
my father throws himself into the scarce research
available. I take life one day at a time now – fly
by the seat of my pants. My father grapples with
his mental control and fear. No new symptoms to
report.

June 1987

● ● ●

Just saw a clinical nutritionist. He was very helpful. He recommended the following supplements:

Breakfast: 3 Tbsp safflower oil, 2 flax tablets, 2 enzymes (before meal), 2 calcium citrate (after meal) nutritional supplement, evening primrose oil (optional)

Lunch: same regimen, minus calcium citrate
Dinner: 2 enzymes, 2 calcium citrate

I had some new numbness begin yesterday. It developed around my right hip. Today, I woke up and it had spread up my side and to my breast and back. Some places, the numbness is more intense than others. Feels like plastic, tight skin, almost fake. Also, I have off balance moments feeling lightheaded and dizzy. It causes slight traces of nausea here and there. Lips will writhe as a strange electric "feeling" comes over me. It is the most

• • •

uncomfortable of all my symptoms. It strikes at freak times with no general pattern then it slowly lessens. I am finding it hard to hide, but I manage. I only have a few more months with the parents before I go back to school. Thank God.

August 1987

Numbness is still lightly present. Now, double vision has hit again. I haven't had this symptom for a while. It envelopes the full range of my vision – not just my right side anymore. Actually, it is on my left side now moving across my range of vision and not as broken up on the right side. It seems to be worse in the morning and evening, especially at far off distances • • • (when I try to focus

64

far off). Riding in a car is terrible! The nutritionist gave me more supplements, but it is only temporary. (8-10 weeks) Additions include: Homozone, Kyodrophilus, Aminoplex, Vitamin M, Citracidal. Because of the compensating for the double vision (turning my neck and holding it in a strange position to lessen or normalize my vision), I have a stiff neck. It really gets stiff about 5:30 pm and stays that way all night until the morning. Talked with the nutritionist and he thinks maybe I have a ph imbalance so he is releasing me from some of the supplements for two weeks. My father thinks this is a waste of time. He has collaborated to begin research with another scientist. He has shut down and is focused solely on MS research. His manic behavior is worsening.

Few weeks later: Double vision still present and even more intense. I am wearing prism glasses for a time in hopes this will subside

• • •

soon. The glasses hurt my eye sockets though. They get tired and achy. They are 18 out of a possible 20. I am holding hope that this too, will pass! Patience isn't a virtue – it is something you learn. I am a master of disguise.

Late August: The double vision has lessened enough that I don't have to wear the glasses. I have a slight focusing problem. The images I view want to split apart, but I am able to pull them back together. I've been hiding it well since I got away to college again. It was hard to hide. I lied to my best friends. I hope they didn't suspect anything. I've started hiding symptoms from my father. He is obsessed with MS.

February 1988

* * *

I have been researching MS as much as possible in a different way than my father. Seems like doctors just suggest that you sit and wait around to see what happens because the disease is unique to each person who has it. The course is unpredictable and I could wake up tomorrow and not walk or not be able to see. One doctor told me to just go home and pretty much give up. I can't do that! I am not wired that way. I am researching alternative therapies that might help. I am exercising and eating a more balanced diet low in fat. To know I can do something to just keep everything else healthy is soothing to my mind. I am writing because I have a strange new symptom. It is very similar to an old one I had about this time last year, but it is not quite as harsh. It is a nauseating dizziness that is characterized and monopolized by rolling chills up my spine and arms. I can say that it is annoying and eerie enough to make me

• • •

shudder and cringe, frozen and mildly paralyzed from its effect. Sometimes it is mild and sometimes it is nasty and intense. It is easy to hide because it is not physical. I just sometimes seem as if I have been hitting the bottle. I am a college student and can blame it on a weekend of partying. If that is the worst anyone thinks, I don't care. Art and writing are my saviors.

July 1988

The hot summer is staggering. I am a limp dishrag. I have been having a new symptom. My hands shake, especially the right hand. It is not a visible shaking, but it affects the function of my hand. My fingers feel stiff and don't want to work together or as fast. I also have an intention tremor. When I go to do

• • •

something with my hands, they start to shake. My father is thick into research and his agitation and bipolar behavior are wearing my mother thin. My family and the gang are going on our annual beach vacation soon. I can't tell Holden or Rory. Something won't let me involve them. I am too fragile and prideful to let them treat me differently. They will, too. I need normalcy to cope and time to figure out what my father is doing. He frightens me with his talks of this new promising treatment. It seems crazy.

Later in July: Have been dying on the beach. I can't take the heat in the afternoon. I have to come in and rest. I just blame it on my fair skin. Have a strange sensation around the left corner of my mouth and lips. It is numb and tingles. It is almost as if I have been to the dentist and had a shot. It makes me feel odd and I catch myself about to drool at times.

● ● ●

August 1988

The shaking in my hands persists and has spread to both hands now. My legs have become mildly numb and rubbery when I walk. I am the only one who notices it, thankfully. The strange feeling that would come over me back in February has returned. It causes a lightheaded feeling that produces chills up and down my spine and arms. It makes me grit my teeth when it washes over me. My land shifts and quick movements or motions of the body cause my equilibrium to wane. It is the terrible heat of this summer. I am heat intolerant.

I met some people from a local MS chapter and they were very helpful. It was hard to watch a few of the volunteers. They had MS, too. I haven't been around anyone who has it, and didn't realize how differently it affects everyone. This one lady was rigid and wobbly

• • •

70

and would blow over in a breeze. Her attitude was awesome even though her body was betraying her. She inspired me. Even her voice sounded choppy as if someone was shaking her. Everyone shared "war stories" and it was a splash of cold water for me. I suppose I don't want to accept that fate. I want to run like hell.

October 1988

I woke up this morning with a case of numbness and tingling from below my breast down. I noticed it after a hot shower and at the time it was mild, yet nastily concentrated, in my torso region. My feet were tingling intermittently, too. Then, the next day, the numbness progressed to a greater intensity, moving from my knees down. The numbness is very heavy, causing my feet and legs to feel

71

tight and like two logs, making walking laborious. The morning and evening seem to be the worst. I haven't had numbness like this in four years. Hopefully, I can keep moving so that it doesn't slow my walking down. Walking seems to keep my feet tingling rather than being totally dead weight numb. I have lots of fatigue from dragging around this lumber yard. Going to call my mother and have her meet me this weekend. She is worried about my father's new associations. He is gone for long periods of time and returns more inward, his lassitude very apparent.

Mid October: The numbness has worsened if that is possible. I have never experienced any loss of feeling, strength, or mobility like this. Everything is tight and feels like logs. I went to the doc and he told me I was having numbness and spasticity that is causing the stiff muscles. They are weak, so they compensate in order to support me by stiffening up. It has

● ● ●

moved up to about mid torso. I also have to urinate much more often than normal. There is a research study for new medications to treat MS. I am considering the study because it can only help me and others like me. I've got to try to quell my father's rapid descent. I can't continue on this course or I will be old by thirty. The only thing holding me back is fear of my father. Fear is nasty and rules me now. I have to tell my mother my fears and get her thoughts.

November 1988

The numbness in my legs has gotten better, yet the intense "dead" feeling has moved to my chest. It is very tight and constricting as if ace bandages are wrapped tightly around my chest – like I'm wearing a girdle 24-7. It causes shortness of breath ... and incredible

73

fatigue. I tire easily. It is hard to exercise, but I have to keep up because it is a major key.

Note: lasted 6 weeks

Christmas Eve 1988

We went to the beach for Christmas this year because dad was AWOL. It was just mom and me. Gulf Shores was a welcome sight, a relief. I sat in the loft with mom. We drank wine and I painted. We shared a lot that night, formed a consensus regarding my father. I was coming off the last exacerbation and feeling much like my old self. I talked with her about the research study and gave her some information about starting therapy. She encouraged me to do it. She begged me to clue in Rory and Holden, to lean on them, but I see they have

• • •

*been flirting with more than friendship. I can't
tell them yet. They are just so perfect to watch.*

Old Ghosts

Rory closed the diary. They had been
taking turns reading it aloud for several hours.
Rory took off her small glasses and rubbed her
tired eyes as she yawned. Holden addressed
her from his corpse position.

"One of my regular guys at Gabby's has
MS. Unless he told you, you'd never know
anything was wrong with him." Holden knew
something had been wrong with Gabrielle. He
had caught her with her guard down many
times and noticed little things that just hadn't
added up.

"This disease is insidious. Gabby didn't
have time to explain. That would be time
wasted. She was racing herself." Rory
understood Gabby's unspoken communication.

● ● ●

Fear that built walls to keep Gabby safe from her MS were similar to the ones Rory had constructed in her own solitary life. It was the only control they had – their own will.

"How did we miss it?" Holden sat up on his elbows now, looking to Rory for affirmation. Rory tapped the journal with her index finger.

"It wasn't for us to see. She didn't want us to know her that way." Rory stared at the journals. She had been avoiding Holden's probing glances all afternoon, keeping her soul glued to the words on paper.

"I'm starving." Holden fell back onto his back again, looking at the gigantic yellow butterfly Gabby had painted on the ceiling.

"I think I need a drink." Rory stood, stretching her back. Holden coveted her arching movements, proud of the prowess that had created the soreness in the first place. "Her

● ● ●

MS was everywhere. Look at her art, her poetry." Holden analyzed the canvas paintings with fresh vision.

"Pain seeps through the cracks we hide. She hid it beautifully." The magnitude of their friend's secret endeared the room. It wasn't as if Gabby had buried a body – it was nobler – she had battled her own body in relative obscurity.

Rory turned abruptly, walking out the door. Holden heard her tuning up with each step down the rickety stairs. The stifling stillness drew him to the window. Outside, the waves crashed concisely. The ninety degree day made the stationary hooded figure stand out amidst the flow of bodies. It turned, blending into the rush. Holden longed to be just one of the beach people saddled like pack mules with umbrellas and ice chests, children swarming them like bees to honey.

* * *

Have We Met?

Gabby's MS diagnosis had thrown Rory and Holden. They were terse and private, second guessing the day of excavations. Rory hadn't returned from her abrupt exit. Holden watched her pace the shoreline, crying. He had needed some air, too, privacy away from this house that was morphing them into crazy people. Holden went up the road to a small shopping square and got them a pizza and beer.

Holden's cursing and the aroma of pepperoni coaxed Rory from the patio. He had cut his palm trying to open a beer, realizing he had forgotten to buy a bottle opener for his no-twist top import. Irritated, he rummaged through drawers of crumbs, rubber bands, forks, and faded business cards and matchbooks. The foraging stopped when he noticed a recent matchbook from Gabby's.

* * *

His mind quickly returned to the window and the hooded stranger.

"You won't find anything of value in those drawers." Rory reached in her purse, handing him a keychain that had a bottle opener on it.

Holden scrutinized the matchbook, nursing his dark beer in large gulps. He knew it wasn't even a year old. He had switched printing companies and they used wooden matches.

Rory served them both a piece of pizza, but just stared at it on the plate. Holden threw the matchbook back into the drawer. Both let each slice get cold, loyally drinking the beer. Keenly trying to loosen their heavy tongues and closing throats.

"Holden, what is your favorite color?"

"Blue. It has always been blue."

"What is mine?" Rory picked at her cold pepperoni.

* * *

"Red. It will always be red." He opened another beer, wondering where she was leading him.

"What was Gabby's favorite color?" Rory reached for Holden's freshly cut palm, caressing it in docile circular motions.

"Yellow," they replied in unison.

"Maybe Gabby loved what we believed her to be?" Rory's eyes were squalid with mystery.

She stroked the corners of his mouth, tenderly tickling his full lips. Holden pulled Rory into his chest, taking her deep into his lungs, only intimate inches from his heart.

Sounds, Faces

Holden awoke at 3 a.m. They had fallen asleep on the stone floor, their bodies tangled. Gabby's reality had made the comfort of a bed zealous and indulgent. He listened to Rory sleep, her snoring sporadic and alcohol

• • •

induced. Beer bottles peppered the empty room like fallen bowling pins. He rubbed her thigh and she rippled responsively to his touch. He loved the way her body couldn't hide the intent her words rationalized. The untouched pizza had begun to smell, so Holden threw it out. In the darkness, Holden fished for the empty beer bottles. Rory's crimson bra surfaced red as a sunset. It personified her, sultriness in the midst of a cool moonlit room.

Holden walked out to the full moon that left the other houses' long shadows looming gloomily, as if mourning with him. They were both processing Gabby's diagnosis differently, yet each owned the sheer shock and anger. He had lived in a bubble for twenty years and now it had just burst. Old, engrained fears began to creep back up Holden's spine. Rory was hiding behind their history. He walked the beach, bleeding skepticism onto the sand. He knew her core,

• • •

the six-year-old she could never hide. The whole disaster was a game of poker. They bet only what they could stand to lose. Rory wasn't giving up much, but he sensed she had much more to lose. He bargained with the waves as they washed in and out at his feet. Angry, he stomped the surf as it funneled around his ankle, running with the tides.

When Holden heard a series of thuds and clicks coming from Gabby's room, he turned toward their beach house. The silhouette of a face, a motionless shadow gawked down on him. He locked eyes with it for an eternal second, its movement static; a ship on the horizon. Holden ran up the boardwalk to the door, finding Rory still asleep, undisturbed. His blood swished loudly in his ears. He went upstairs and jostled the doorknob of Gabrielle's room. It was still locked. He fished for the key deep in his jeans pocket, quickly releasing the lock. He hit the light switch,

● ● ●

poking his head into the light, his vision adjusting as he scrutinized the room. At first glance, everything appeared the same. He stepped into the window, assuming the shadow's posture when a few stray, broken beads that had hung from Gabby's closet door crunched loudly underfoot.

Experiments

January 1990

With my mother's support, I am going to be part of a clinical trial for possible MS medications. It will be injections given every other day. They will study me over two years. There is a placebo group that doesn't know if they are on the medicine or not, but I was told that I will definitely be on it. Am nervous, but with some very serious new symptoms, I feel it is worth a try. The disease has to be worse.

• • •

First shot: I gave it to myself in the stomach and reacted rather violently to it, but the major side effects lessened by morning. It left me with a headache, mild nausea, and quite tired. I have to take this shot every other day.

Many shots later: Tolerating this medicine well. Have had some chills and muscle stiffness. Symptoms seem to be lessening some. I am feeling more like myself. Have more energy than before.

February 1990

The numbness has considerably worsened the past few weeks. My body is numb all over, particularly my trunk area – breasts to waist. It is a tight, constricting girdle effect. My legs from just above my knees down are numb and intensely heavy. My right hand predominately, too. Bowel and bladder function impaired. I'm

● ● ●

tired of its morphing and am ready for it to relent.

My mother decided to share some of her demons with me today. I noticed that she was bruised when I came home from school for the weekend. She had first told me she fell.
She fell right into my father's fist. He beat her and drugged her for days. He caught her snooping in his research journals. She has been listening on the other line to his phone conversations. He's working with some pretty shady people not just scientists. I fear for our safety. He is obsessed. I am going to call Rhett for advice since he is about to become a lawyer.

"Damn it, Lexie. Why didn't you just leave?" Holden groaned with scorn. He tossed the journal like a Frisbee, bouncing it off the wall. A few stray pages that had been wedged in the middle boomeranged back at their feet.

* * *

"John was a crazy genius. He must have really had something exceptionally appalling that made them stay." Rory fidgeted with Gabby's red wig, wondering what solace she must have found in pretending to be someone else.

"Lexie told me to trust her after Gabby's death...I never fully did. I hated her for a long time." He closed his eyes and fished through forgotten words and memories.

"We had no control over this." Rory's words were tactile and cruel.

"But *it* had control over *us*." Holden rubbed his eyelids with frenzied fatigue. He was left with only guilt and helplessness.

"Ok, then, what would *you* have done?" Defensiveness surfaced in Rory's fluid tone.

"I would have gotten them out of there and shot that bastard between the eyes." His neck flushed a dark cherry.

* * *

"No, you wouldn't. You have no idea what you would have done in that situation unless it was happening to you. You can hate her for not doing it the way *you* would, but be grateful for her sacrifice. She was just being a good mother." Rory's lip quivered.

"It was my life, too. I had no control or say. So I don't have to *accept* or like her sacrifices." Rory moved into Holden's personal space, wanting him to touch and comfort her. But, Holden went pitiless.

"Asking you to come into their life with this situation would just further their anxiety. They used distance to protect all involved." Holden denied her touches, grabbing her wrist.

"*They*...I thought *their* hands were tied... or do you mean *Rhett*?" Rory's pregnant pause tightened Holden's grip. His mistrust was palpable.

● ● ●

"Rhett had to minimize the things he couldn't control, Holden."

"That's a crock of crap. He maximized the things he could."

"Rhett was a good lawyer. He used to tell his clients *you may not like me, but you can trust me to protect your best interests like my own.*"

Holden inhaled long and exhaled just as labored, releasing her wrist. Rory could almost feel the oxygen being sucked from the room in troubling gulps.

"Oh, come on Rory. You and I both know lawyers master crocodile tears." Holden studied Rory's poker face. She fell silent when forced to take his or Rhett's side on anything.

"I never said lawyers were sincere, just effective." She was overly passive to his aggression. To Holden, Rory was a puzzle

* * *

missing that one key piece, in effect, tainting the true view.

The sun moved behind a cloud as if closing a window shade and the room's vibrant landscape fell colorless. Out the window on the horizon, the clouds conspired against the sun. Rory picked up the journal, placing the loose pages on the desk. She gently positioned it back on Holden's lap, reminiscent of how a teacher directs her student to do his homework. Rory's mute coercion seemed to be the missing puzzle piece. Yet, Holden didn't know how to make it fit.

April 1990

Rhett has become my confidante. I've shared everything with him regarding my father. I even told him about my MS which is huge because I have virtually told no one. He

* * *

has his mafia connected uncle watching my father closely. My mother gave me some photocopied bits of his research and I gave them to Rhett to study. Although this conflicts me, I trust Rhett and feel he truly can protect all of us like no one else could. He will involve no one else.

Later: Rhett took me to the doc today. I'm taking a week of steroid treatments, my first ever. My legs got very weak and gave out from under me yesterday and I fell and scraped my knees. Rhett helped me clean my cuts and took me to dinner. He made me feel like a lady.

Later still: Steroids helped. I am getting my energy back, but I am still numb. It is so intense. I use a cane a lot in private because my legs are not yet strong enough to carry me. I have to balance my energy. Legs get stiff at the end of the day from the normalcy I try to keep up.

● ● ●

June 1990

I am going away to the beach house with my family and Rory and Holden are joining us. I haven't seen Holden and Rory in over a year, but I couldn't exclude them because it would seem suspicious. They have been hot and heavy dating, have their lives to lead. I am so very happy for them and have hoped they would finally realize they are beautifully made for each other. I can't wait until they make pretty babies. I'll be a good aunt.

I am really tolerating the new experimental medication better. I have more energy. I don't know if it is the medicine or just hope. I could be at the pioneering door of something for such an ambiguous disease. I feel wonderful. Better than I have in years. Maybe because Rhett has been treating me like a princess. I don't know how Rory and Holden will handle this ... façade we hide behind. Rhett and I are pretending to be more than friends so Rhett can get a bit closer to my father. John likes Rhett and it gives Rhett a reason to be around in order to snoop. I like having him around. I'm starting to understand Rory and Holden's years of crushing.

Beach Day 1: We just got settled in Gulf Shores. I am apprehensive and full of strange emotions today. I was eager to hit the beach alone. My father has been acting strange, almost sad. He hugged me a lot longer than normal when I left. Any hug from him is odd. He seemed very depressed and weepy. It makes me anxious. I keep looking over my shoulder. I fear retaliation of some kind. Holden and Rory just arrived.

Beach Day 2: I am very tired. Traveling is so hard on me, but always worth it. Most of my symptoms are at bay, but I feel calm before another storm. Something new is coming – mark my word. Rhett took me to lunch. We

• • •

walked the beach and he explained some of my father's associations. It is now a dangerous game. Rhett is so charming that he makes me feel bold and strong. I could fall in love with a man like him. Holden and Rory have been out on the sailboat all day. They haven't seen Rhett and we hope to hide him as long as possible. My mother says to tell them about our situation. I am considering it.

Beach Day 3: I received a phone call tonight. It was frightening. The voice said nothing, just breathed oddly. I'm being watched.

Beach Day 4: I told Rhett about the call. He was incredibly quiet and nervous, insisting on seeing me. We met at the boat dock and Rhett shared John's diaries and patient files he had stolen from the beach house. Father did a lot of experimenting on MS patients and now has shifted his focus from finding a cure to something entirely different. His new patients

* * *

are those who are terminal. He wrote in some of his research notes that "they are insignificant and disposable". He is toying with some sort of undetectable death drug and cloaking it under MS research funding. He is due to meet with terrorists - when he has successfully finished a final test – at week end.

I fear having MS for the first time.

Day 5: I woke up with spasticity and numbness in my legs. I had to privately use my cane again so on one would notice. I can't show weakness of any kind and sometimes traveling affects me days or weeks later.

Later: It was time. Rhett came by and gave me $5000 cash. We've really bonded, shared so much. He's my best friend right now. I kissed him. I think it surprised him. I know he can't love me the same, but I have nothing to offer him for his help other than my devotion. I fear that my father knows our plans. We have to get all his ... research or I am *afraid of what awaits all of us. I have to move as fast as my weak legs will take me, tonight.*

Final Entry: If something happens to me, I must have this written to clarify my father's intentions. Rhett's investigation into my father's past revealed his days as a resident and his experimental drug tests on unsuspecting, terminal patients. Seems my father also dabbled in trying to bring people that were dead back to life. He was unsuccessful in his attempts. His experimental medications didn't work. Some of the research won him acclaim. He was bold and cutting edge, but everyone mistook his bravado, didn't know about his mental state until his patients started dying rapidly. I remember my father being taken to a facility when I was very young. Rhett produced a report by one of his therapists from the original evaluations. "He was always working to 'be like God' in manipulating life, fascinated with what happened when we

● ● ●

died..." As John Vansant progressed with his studies, his mental descent escalated, he became more depressed and hopeless. This has turned into calculated anger. He stated that the madness of his profession made him want to kill all the 'poor terminal bastards' suffering needlessly. This is when he began putting his deathbed patients out of their misery. It made him 'God'."

Raging Rain

Rain came in sheets, raging against their beach house all day. Small nooks had formed where the house had settled, allowing brief bursts of water to worm in through the doors and windows. Holden had pulled his mattress into the living room adjacent to the wall, creating a makeshift couch.

● ● ●

"Remember how we used to sneak out in this kind of rain to swim? Gabby led the charge so we never got in trouble." Rory flinched as thunder rumbled in angry, explosive fits, punching the wind with a growl.

"There was no such thing as rain on the beach...or MS, or crazy fathers...or your brother." Holden closed the journal he had been reading aloud. He tossed it into Rory's lap.

"You skipped ahead a year, you know? You are the kind of reader that wastes the last chapter first and I hate that." Rory's red glasses rested low on her nose. Her hair was a wavy mess, complements of the humidity. It tussled with her fingers as she forced it over her ear.

"You and anticipation need to get a room. I just wanted the end result." Holden rubbed his eyes, yawning wearily. His tone had soured

• • •

with Gabby's words of Rhett's involvement.

"Why are you so against the reasons?" Rory flipped to the middle of the book, her fingers nimble and concise.   Her passive aggressiveness goaded Holden.

"The *reason* she's dead, Rory, is because she trusted your brother." The wind gust peppered the panes of the old glass with sharp sand. Holden dropped his head back against the wall, breaking the anxious nothingness and still of his curt tongue.

"You shouldn't go there." Rory gritted her teeth, fidgeting with the ruby ring that hung around her neck.

"Christ Rory, what are we reading this for? Does it give you closure? It just makes me suspicious." Holden craved a cigarette.
He hadn't smoked one in ten years.

"It makes me empathize and understand what Gabby went through." Rory just picked at

• • •

the stitching on the mattress, prying the stray ones loose.

"Gabby leaned on your brother rather than tell you and me, yet we still got screwed.
It pisses me off and I can't understand why it doesn't bother you?" Holden pushed, waiting for her to pull.

"I'm sure Gabby had her reasons." Rory didn't even tug.

"You are hiding behind your brother again!" Holden's voice boomed, harmonizing with the rain, an audible symphony of word and sound.

Rory fell silent, her eyes on the journals.

"Fine - I think Rhett was the scourge of the earth. I won't apologize for my feelings. He fed on your weakness. He brainwashed you both. Fuck him." Holden turned and punched a hole in the wall the size of a grapefruit.

● ● ●

"My God, Holden. Gabby suffered and died and you just blame Rhett?" Rory screamed at Holden vehemently, ripping the chain off her neck and throwing it in his face.

She had her face in her hands, her moplike hair hiding her anger as she stomped to the door, blaring obscenities with each step. Thunder vibrated the floor under her bare feet. She reached instinctively for the doorknob, weighing the storm's power in the dark of dusk.

"I know what you're doing, Rory." Holden stood, taking two steps toward her.

"No, you don't." Rory strangled the door knob before releasing it.

They appeared trapped by the storms of their past, both natural and manmade. Holden took Rory's hand, staring into her resilient sea green eyes. He had failed to puncture her walls with force or anger. Thunder rang out the clouds with a firm grip, sending the showers

● ● ●

down in short cruel bursts. Holden hurled the door open, steadfastly gripping

Rory's fingers, insanely coaxing her into the blinding rain. They ran hand in hand to the ocean's edge, diving into the salt water that strung their eyes and faces. They fought the bullishness of the waves, lured by the seduction of finding the crest and bodysurfing on the water's thrust into the shore. The undertow vacillated their sandy footing, the unseen enemy bobbing them like buoys.

Rory slowly crawled to shore seeing Holden's lofty stature like a lighthouse amidst the bleak night. He grabbed Rory's hand, pulling her into his momentum and they raced the beach with the rain.

● ● ●

Emotional Roller Coasters

Rory awoke the next morning to the smell of coffee, Holden's heavy footsteps, and finally the broken strumming of a guitar. They mingled with Rory's flashes from their swim, the waves and guitar in sync. They had returned to the house, soaking the flooring with sea water and sand, adding to its familiar history. Holden had pushed her onto the mattress, horse play from so many summers past. He tickled her, dominating her wet, slippery skin and she screamed in rebellion so loud there was no way the neighbors hadn't heard it. Holden tried to put his hand over her mouth, but Rory strong-armed him with strength that mirrored her resolve. So, Holden conceded by tenderly brushing his whiskery cheek to hers, signaling a truce for now.

Rory heard her cell phone chime from her purse, a missed call. She knew the caller, had to return it. She slipped onto the deck and

● ● ●

made the call as the sun began its orange ascent through muddled cloud banks.

"I'm alive and well if you thought me dead." She replied to his covert hello.

"I know you are ok. I was just wondering what was happening. Is there anything I need to know?" She wondered where he was as loud, sporadic chatter overtook his voice on occasion.

"I would say we have reconciled some issues, but there is still a lot on the table." Rory bit her cuticles.

"You haven't told him?" Exasperation masked his disappointment.

"The stuff with Gabby is amazingly frightening. It isn't the right time."

"That's just an excuse...tell him."

"I'll share more when I can talk." Rory abruptly ended the conversation.

● ● ●

The storms had passed, leaving dark, odd-shaped clouds resembling pewter balloon animals. People were beginning to scatter onto the sand once again. Umbrellas were opening every fifteen minutes. Holden watched Rory on the patio, talking on her cell phone. Her facial expressions were visibly curt, her brow wrinkled. As he moved from the window, he caught a glimmer of what appeared to be his hooded figure. He turned around quickly, only spying a sea of beach people; his paranoia inventing lurking monsters.

Holden resumed the guitar and a dull burn brewed in his throat. He hummed as he strummed on Gabby's guitar, playing the meandering chords Gabby had penciled on her make shift staff. She had been forced to create above Rory's written words.

"Morning." Rory's brow hadn't relaxed. The phone call had curdled her mood.

● ● ●

"I found some of Gabby's music. I was trying to play it. It has been a while since I picked up a guitar." Holden plucked at the strings awkwardly.

"This looks like your handwriting, though." Holden snarled his nose and squinted.

"You mean you can't read it?" The corner of Rory's lip curled.

"It was pretty brutal." Holden handed Rory the tattered page.

"Easy, I haven't had my coffee." Rory read the words.

Holden began to play.

"When you strum the guitar in the way Gabby suggests, it sounds haunting and kind of hypnotic, not typical Gabby."

Holden's dexterity was choppy, but eventually he mastered its repetitive strum.

● ● ●

The once absent sunlight now energized the dust particles floating in the air. The dust danced to the tune like a ghost in their midst. The faint freckles on Rory's nose appeared harsh and brash as the color left her face.

Old Decembers

Your world can fall to pieces, leave you in the cold
But old December mornings never die or grow old.
Just one millisecond looking into your soul
Will bring me back around, make me take control.

Refrain: In the dark and lonely corners you are always my love, my friend. It isn't an illusion, we will never end. Say it will never end.

I feel you moving through me like a wave onto the shore
And I find the keys to pieces of you yet fumble at the door.
I want you to help me understand the strangeness of your charms

• • •

For I don't think I'm real anymore – it's cold outside your arms.

Refrain

I've searched every corner trying to find the light
But the blind truly feel the world, never missing sight.
I find that time and fear keep me just beyond your reach.
For an ounce of you is ample and somehow meant to teach.

"I can't believe this...I wrote this song *after* Gabby's death...after I lost you." Rory's pallor began weakening her. "I told him to let *me* handle this..."

"Who is *he*? Is it the one I've seen following us?" Holden set the guitar aside as if it burned his fingertips.

"What *man* following us?" Rory fell to her knees and began to hyperventilate,

● ● ●

gasping for the missing oxygen Holden had consumed the day before.

Holden stepped on more fallen beads. He rushed to the window, searching the small patches of beach goers. He found their hooded stranger moving slowly south. His large footsteps were well-defined in the smooth sand the storm erased the night before. The stranger's trail had originated right beneath them.

Holden knew Gabby's closet was offset and accessible from the lower floors. He scooted the chest out of Gabby's closet, fumbling around the floorboards until he found the grooved opening, springing the trap door. Tied up methodically was a wood and rope ladder that had once been attached to Gabby's tree house.

"Jesus Christ, Rory!" Holden closed the trap door. "We're being tailed."

● ● ●

"It's not what you think Holden…*please* let me explain." Rory's voice was compromised, yet her eyes bled guilt and shame.

Holden took the stairs three at a time, rattling the old door hinges. He headed south, running in spurts until he spotted the figure 100 yards on the horizon, running rhythmically, alone in the more secluded and empty sand. He was wearing shorts and a hooded vest. When the man stopped running and began walking, Holden sprinted, closing the gap. Holden pummeled him into the sand face first with his adrenalin and stature.

The man struggled briefly, but Holden's two-handed grip on the back of his neck paralyzed his fight. Holden flipped him over and pulled his hood off, revealing his sandy young face. The man had thick, wavy dark hair. He was pissed off, spitting sand out of his mouth in ⚬ ⚬ ⚬ chunks. That blister in Holden's throat began to simmer. Holden had every intention of punching this punk in the nose and throttling a confession out of his silent lungs. Yet, when he looked into his clear green eyes, Holden's fists oddly betrayed him. The two men stared at each other, frozen and conflicted.

"Who do you work for?" Holden pressed the younger man's shoulders into the sand. The stranger was pigheaded, breathing heavily, his glare indignant.

"Who are you?!" Holden manhandled the lean, solid frame, roughing him up. The young man remained inflexible, rebutting Holden.

"Holden…stop….this is the man who wrote the music to my song." Rory had caught up to them and was now bent over, breathless.

● ● ●

"Who in the hell are you to be skulking around our house?" Holden pushed on his lungs again in interrogation.

"He is my son...*your* son, William Holden." Rory's voice was tenacious, her words all-consuming.

Holden scrutinized his twenty-year-old newborn, trying to process the words *your son.* The white noise of the waves fueled his manic anger.

Holden unhanded Will, turning his anger to Rory. William scurried beside his mother. Holden's fists were clinched, merely inches between their defensiveness.

"What in the hell have you done?" Holden swung wildly at Rory, but Will caught Holden's wrist just as his fingertips grazed Rory's neck, his green eyes as pervasive as his mother's. Betrayal gawked from the mouths of hungry seagulls overhead.

● ● ●

Seconds to Years

Holden ran away from them both, from any breathing thing, further and further down the secluded beach. Large tears rushed his flushed face. He ran all the way to Ft. Morgan, stopping at some old ruins that had a flight of stairs that led nowhere, mocking his journey. He walked half way up collapsing on the cold, mossy stone. A verbal tirade of garbage from his soul calmed to gibberish as salty tears ran down his fingertips, releasing him from the hurt, anger, and cold, calculated madness he had harbored for decades.

He covered his eyes so as not to see the minuscule fragments of himself that were dying. His mind flashed bittersweet suppositions, years he had missed. This stairwell was now a sealed tomb, housing the remains of his youth that had failed him.

● ● ●

Holden had been missing all afternoon. His sight was bleary from blinding tears. He had composed himself and begun a very surreal walk back to the beach house, unsure of his tongue or fists, both hardened to stone. When he got to the beach house, he paused, inhaling salt air into his lungs, oxygenating his wits. He opened the old door whose hinges he had compromised earlier. Rory was standing in the empty kitchen, whimpering with talented agony.

"I wasn't sure you'd come back." Rory wouldn't face him.

"Where's William?" Holden cased the room like a zombie thirsting blood; his eyes piss holes of despondency.

"He is at Madison's." Rory stared at the ruby ring that glistened from the mattress.

Holden lumbered into his room. Rory knew he was gathering his bag, heard him

● ● ●

sifting, odd and end packing sounds. He rejoined her, tossing his duffle bag into the center of the empty house. He had changed his clothes and shoes back to his old street self.

"Holden, for what it's worth...I didn't know Will was here watching us. I told him about Gabby's trap door when he was a boy." Rory's tenor was cautious and probing.

"I thought we were being stalked...then you were talking on the phone..." Holden stomped the mattress and the ruby ring bounced and rolled to Rory's feet.

Holden didn't want to hear her speak anymore of William as a boy or their life without him.

"Rory, I have to leave. I can't look at you. I can't hear this. I don't want to hear your fuzzy logic. 1990 is dead to me." Holden's face knotted into the demons that had

● ● ●

plagued him, dark rings reflected the bleakness in his pupils.

"So, I've just been in love with a memory of us?" Rory crossed her arms, her walls secure; her face porcelain and stony.

"*You* came here knowingly deceiving me. *You* made me believe in us, in a future." Holden poked Rory's chest bullishly with his index finger.

Rory slammed her palm on the worn countertop.

"I never led you to believe anything, Holden. 1990 is dead to you, then get out. I won't apologize for the past." She tossed his belongings toward the door.

Holden glared at her in disgust.

Holden slammed the door squarely in her face, shattering their reunion. She heard his car engine crank and just like that, he was gone again, a memory.

. . .

Music Man

Rory crashed on the mattress with a wounded plop. The past two weeks of time spent with Holden floated like bubbles above her head. They popped just as magically, magnifying her sudden loneliness. She didn't hear Will rapping lightly. The volume of the conversations in her head overtook everything else. He entered sheepishly, examining the infamous house in a different slant from his mother's stories.

Will sat beside his mother on the mattress, picking at the old name tag that was dry and cracking through the word Sealy.

Rory rolled Holden's prized ruby ring between her index fingers over and over and over. Their breaths were white noise to their numbed brains. Both searched for ways to cope with the day's reversal.

● ● ●

"How did you figure out I wrote the music?" Will had underestimated his mother's innate attention to his every detail.

"I wrote those words *after* Gabby died. I knew she didn't write that music. I remember you playing that string of chords relentlessly. It is beautiful. You got that gift from Holden." Rory put her arm around Will's long torso, noticing a new stringency in his posture.

"I'm sorry for following you both. I just...I needed to see you together...make sure you were OK." Will wasn't a good liar. Rory felt his caginess.

"And we wouldn't be OK because..." Rory left the sentence open-ended, prodding him to finish it properly.

Will stood, lowered his chin and placed his hands in his pockets. A gesture he had done a thousand times as a boy when he was about to make a confession and beg for leniency. Rory

• • •

crossed her arms and puckered her brow, primed for disapproval, yet knowing he could never disappoint her.

"You remember when I went to Washington? Well, I didn't go to look at schools. I got a letter from Lexie Vansant and I went out to meet her. She was dying." Rory's shoulders fell in surprise. Her silence ushered him to continue.

"Lexie asked me to make sure you got Gabby's journals. Rhett had them. She said that they would explain *everything* to the two of you." Skepticism bled from Will's voice.

"So you are the reason Madison called me with Gabby's journals?" Rory's words were pronounced eloquently, yet sweetly gritty from a bit of disbelief.

"I wasn't trying to hide anything from you. Lexie didn't swear me to secrecy or

● ● ●

anything... I just needed to do this my way…for my own understanding."

"I can respect that." Rory had taught him to shoulder his choices well.

"*Did* the journals explain *everything*?" Will's style of commanding answers mirrored his father's.

"The secrets Gabby kept about her health and her father were pretty unnerving, a bit earth-shattering, but no dangers we didn't eventually find out. *Everything* is an ambiguous word."

"Then, why did Uncle Rhett have the journals? They have to be dangerous or worth something?" Their green eyes dueled for reasons and logic.

"I can't answer that." Rory understood Will's helplessness, his need to control his past and uncover the all inclusive *everything*. It was why she had stolen every ounce of Holden's

● ● ●

air, her own need to steer *everything* to a good place just once.

"I just feel there is more to this." Will's frustrations bubbled to the surface, simmering loudest in the things he didn't say.

"You may be right, but everyone involved in this is dead. I think we should move ahead rather than barter with old ghosts." Rory spoke from a place of weary wisdom. She was feeling the fallout from reopening the past with Gabby's journals.

"Do you think my father will come back to us?" Will was a contradiction, a man child. His body was strong and adult, but his emotions were frazzled and raw.

"I've done all I can do. I made my intentions clear, son." Rory stared at the rubies on the ring that shone purposefully in her eyes.

"I haven't had a choice. I want a chance." Rory placed the ruby ring in the palm of

● ● ●

Will's hand. She closed his fingers around it tightly, kissing his fist.

"Then, take *your* chance. Don't wait for him to come back, William. Go to him. Go *forward*."

* * *

August 2010

Going Solo

Rory had been repainting all the rooms downstairs, for the past few weeks. She rolled the final touches to the tall, empty living room walls with long up and down swipes just like Gabby had taught her. Walls were just large canvases. She had chosen clay colors for the other rooms that reflected the multiple shades of sand and the harmony she felt being engaged in the present. Maybe Rory had chosen a shade of red paint for the large room because it mirrored the mid- August heat or maybe she just felt angry and frustrated because of what this particular room meant to her? The rusty red was warm and commanding, opposing the once cool, complacent influence of vanilla. It changed the ambiance for new memories to be made in the space.

● ● ●

In the long solitary evenings, Rory had started writing essays and poetry, rekindling her private joys. Painting and cleaning the beach house had focused Rory's mind since Will's departure for Breckenridge, giving her monotony to line out her life. Rory's newfound limbo felt different than in the past. She had control of the choices. Only after Rhett's death did Rory realize how disabling his protection had truly been to her sanity. Rory now considered finding a new purpose. She had journalism and communication degrees that she had fought Rhett to utilize often editing work at a small university press in Philadelphia after Will was born. It had kept her plugged into the world, not sacrificing every stitch of her identity no matter how sizable a bank roll Rhett had promised.

Rory grunted as she looked from the beautiful red room to her biggest challenge, the kooky kitchen. The cabinets needed cleaning

● ● ●

out and scrubbing. It had become the catch-all room because of its storage space. It had nooks and crannies to shove years of unused gizmos that could easily go unnoticed for decades. She pulled a large trash can into the middle of the kitchen and started at the furthest corner. Rory unearthed mismatched decks of cards, old wadded-up newspapers, deteriorating boxed puzzles, an airbrushed can holder with Gabby's name on it, and old guest books signed by visitors back in the late eighties when the Vansants rented the house out. These things were singular. Rory couldn't throw them away. She wished she had found these before Will had left. She would have given the keepsakes to Holden for his bar. She stacked them into a pile and would store them in Gabby's vintage bedroom.

The cabinet made an L in an odd place that seemed to collect the circular things that could roll. There were golf balls, batteries, an

* * *

ancient empty can of W-D40, a random wooden shrimp skewer, and a dusty, empty wine bottle. Rory examined each item, waiting for them to tell their story. The WD40 had leaked and the batteries were corroded and covered in a furry growth. The golf balls had a faded logo *Gulf Shores Plantation*. She put them in the save pile. The empty wine bottle was crusted with sand. Rory smeared at the filthy label, instantly deducing it had been a bottle of wine from the Vansant's stash, similar to the one she and Holden had drained like teenagers their first night back to the beach. The label was faint, but she made out the year – 1990. Something foreign was lodged inside. Rory fished it out with the wooden shrimp skewer. It was a rolled up piece of white notebook paper.

June 1990

My MS has been so unstable. My legs keep failing - I feel so helpless at times. I am in the

• • •

middle of a crisis in my life and my body won't function. I need my legs; legs that betray me - a body that is attacking itself. My body is teaching my spirit a few lessons. My haunt is my disease. My peace is the union of the spirit and body. It is amazing how one fuels the other. I know I am more than my body. Anyone who doesn't believe that has never truly lived or had to rise above their failing shell. My father is coming for me next. He is waiting and watching us all. I will win because I have accepted my fate. I don't fight to control my life, I just live it 'til it is through with me - Time to fly – until hello...

Rory sat cross-legged, mentally thumbing through the wine bottles of Gabby's past. Gabby had become somewhat of a gypsy when she went off to college, her contact sporadic and often bizarre. That made sense now that Rory knew about Gabby's MS. Holden and Rory never knew

● ● ●

when Gabby would materialize, just like her unpredictable disease. If she was coming, Gabby never asked if she could stay, she imposed ruthlessly just as her MS silently did.

Gabby's parents raised her with an appreciation for wine. They drank it with two of their three daily meals. Shortly before Gabby made an appearance, a bottle of wine from the current year, sometimes cheap and mostly trendy, would show up on their door step. It was considered her fair warning. When Gabby left, they'd find an empty wine bottle. Gabby hated goodbyes.

Until hello she'd pen and leave sticking out the bottle's neck…always relenting quietly along with her secrets. Rory flung the bottle across the faded linoleum flooring and it rolled in slow, vicious circles. This might have been Gabby's way of trying to tell them all goodbye that final summer. Gabby's coded pleas were buried even deeper than her disease.

● ● ●

Invitations

Rory kneaded the roller, watching the diluted rusty red paint roll down the bathtub drain. It seemed to thin-out a bit with each squeeze, but it was gummy, she had let it sit too long before rinsing. The kitchen had stolen her attention, and the roller was ruined with crunchy flecks of paint. As Rory shut off the water, she thought she heard the faint sound of an ancient doorbell used only by unexpected guests. Light rapping was followed by a fervently concerned grip jiggling the doorknob.

"Rory…are you here?" Rory knew those soft, concerted syllables. It was Madison Peacock, her former sister-in-law.

"I'm coming!" Rory bellowed and her vocals seemed to bounce more evenly off the fresh paint.

• • •

Rory unlocked the door slowly with gooey fingers and Madison turned the knob over. A denim blue eyeball attached to a two foot frame peered curiously around the door. Madison ushered Peck, her toddler, inside quickly and he wrinkled his nose at the smell of the pungent paint.

"I just wanted to check in on you, see how you are doing… if you needed anything."
Rory had always loved Madison's gregarious demeanor. Her crystal blue eyes emboldened her new found happiness with another man, another family she had somehow created after Rhett's death.

"William put you up to this. He's checking his guilty conscience through you?" Rory smiled sheepishly as she watched Madison corral her rampant toddler with graceful, sure motions.

"No, I guess it's my own guilty conscience. Rhett ●●● never did play family very well and I suppose it rubbed off." Madison's honesty caught Rory off guard. They had spoken little since Rhett's death, had both just wanted to make a clean break from the drama.

"I guess I am alright, considering everything. There are so many things left undone. Who am I kidding? You understand having your life change overnight." Rory kept her hands busy as to avoid eye contact with Madison, but she could feel Madison's stare eating through her skull. Madison was always a psychologist.

"Things never really changed overnight, Rory. They just never were what they appeared with Rhett." Rory focused on the wine bottle briefly, knowing Madison was studying her reaction. Madison noticed the wine bottle, but her young son's curiosity diverted her eyes. Peck was fascinated with Rory's fluid fingers.

"Little man, you make me miss *my* little man." Peck poked the wet roller Rory had set aside to drip dry, ••• squealing   in delight. Rory pinched the roller and his giggle was hearty like a seasoned old man.

Peck snatched the wet roller and ran around in circles preparing to flail it around his head, chanting in his oddly deep, male resonance when Madison pried it from his chubby fists, crisis averted. It was her specialty.

"How do you handle a toddler?" Rory was tired from merely observing Peck's reservoir of never-ending oomph.

"You play the cards you are dealt. Peck is a refreshing pause in my very…eventful journey." Madison's life was once a nonstop rollercoaster that Rhett instigated and stirred fastidiously. Children would have never factored into his equation.

"I played my hand, Madison. All I have now is time…and pieces…" Rory scrubbed the rust from her fingers. It was reminiscent of blood, dying the cracks and lines of her palms.

● ● ●

"I shouldn't be boring you with this mess…"

"Peck has a birthday this week. *Come –* have dinner with us...let's *play* family." Madison had always milked her verbs resiliently, carrying life vests in her back pocket.

"I'd like that." Rory toweled her paint stained hands leaning into Madison's compassion. Peck had channeled his wanderlust, bobbling toward the two painted canvases waiting to be hung. The bold colors and thick textures beckoned his very tactile existence. Peck looked to Madison, his restless fingers behind his back.

"Mine." Peck was adamant and sure he knew Gabby's twenty year old abstracts. He ran his tiny finger over the rough forked paint with a pianist's fluidity.

"No, Peck."

"Yes, mine!" Madison pulled his hands away. She picked him up as he began grunting and whining.

* * *

"I think we'd better go. The natives are getting restless. I'll call you about dinner…and please, let's keep in touch *this* time." Madison smiled convivially before closing the door.

Rory hated hammering the nails into freshly painted walls. Or, maybe it was because these walls were reminiscent of those cold empty ones in that tiny condo twenty years ago. Rory had nothing to fill them with and Madison had brought her these paintings of Gabby's that she had found. These paintings had become the one constant link to her history and now a precious piece of her future. How many times had

Madison closed that door to Rhett's apartment in Philadelphia in the same manner, as she pealed a young William from Madison's attention? Madison was always generous even though Rory and Will's situation had been one of the many silent strains on Madison and Rhett's new marriage.

● ● ●

The Party

Rory walked barefooted, letting the crusty August sand crunch under her toes. The established walk of this beach had always held a different meaning with each visit. September beckoned new winds, new shifts in thinking and disposition. The anticipation of the new, the hints and subtle nuances blanketed the old with promises; loss and repair walked hand in hand. She remembered summers past and dropping dreams into the ocean like pennies in the vastest wishing well with souls that were now the shadows she cast. The summer wind streaked tears through her laugh lines. Tears that seemed to come on like a virus. She lingered at times working to dissolve the lump in her throat that had now metastasized.

Rory heard the squealing of girls and boys as she approached Madison's boardwalk. A kite flew effortlessly on a ... specially designed hitching post. She watched figures knit behind the windows in the soft orange lamp light of

Madison's home. Hamburgers unmistakably cooked on the grill. The smell was somehow offputting. As she grew closer, a tall man's visible salt and pepper head moved behind the grill, flipping the lid open as he checked the meat. He saw Rory coming and called to Madison who appeared out of the sea of strangers. Madison introduced the tall man as her husband, Houston.

Peck could be heard first stomping then chuckling deeply in a distant part of the house with other children. Madison's nine-year-old daughter, Hannah Beth, helped fill ice glasses in the kitchen. Rory had only learned of this biological niece after Rhett died and Madison adopted her as her own; just one more stolen part of their shared family's history. Hannah looked up at Rory with Rhett's inherited blue eyes as she smiled shyly, sniffing out this new stranger in the room. "Aunt Lane," Hannah whispered to a dark-

* * *

eyed woman who materialized like vapor, exchanging guarded pleasantries while helping Hannah, their mannerisms indistinguishable.

Hannah yelled "Daddy," dropping her scrutiny as a rugged man in work boots walked through the screen door, searing proof that DNA didn't constitute love and family.

The crowd was small and intimate, made up of chosen family with lots of colorful loose odds and ends. The room was a patchwork quilt of promise that worked, complimenting the family tree. Parents of the other toddlers clung to the corners of the rooms with the furniture. They chattered low, sipping wine or beer. The kids moved like a train on a track weaving through the adults. Madison's home was reminiscent of a Vansant summer. Even the houses had similar architecture for their time.

Madison tried to guide Rory to an unoccupied intimate corner, out of the way of nosy ears and ... shrieking toddlers.

Rory noticed how Madison's decorating tastes were more simple and eclectic than in her former life. As they maneuvered, a canvas painting textured in moody blues dominated Rory's periphery. The artist had signed and dated it in a sideways fashion. Rory tilted her head, deciphering the scrawled *Brie 2008*.

"This is unique." Madison watched Rory's eyes fixate and focus like her brother's once did, performing a genetic mental gymnastics of deductions.

"I got that from a local gallery in Gulf Shores. Grace Christy Alexander. You should go by sometime."

Rory fell silent. As they continued to the corner, Madison offered Rory something to drink, but she wrinkled her nose, declining. Rory bowed her head. She was visibly disconnected, her emotions bouncing like a kite on a string.

"You've got a lovely place, a real family.

● ● ●

I am happy for you, Madison…I'm sorry I just haven't been myself lately. I've repainted the house and cleaned everything…" Rory felt warm tears building.

"I know you're lost in uncertainty right now. Will was always so protective of you." Madison had loved Will like her own son. "Thank you for always caring for William Holden…for tolerating our intrusion into your life for all those years." Peck lumbered toward Rory, wrapping his quick hands around her legs. Rory ran her fingers through his thick mop of hair, his head oversized for his tiny body.

"You and Will are both easy to love." Madison reached for Rory's hand and Peck lifted his arms to Rory, wiggling his fingers, wanting to be on her hip. Rory lifted Peck and he gave her a slobbery kiss.

"It was your life back then, too. It's still *your* life… now more than ever."   Rory

* * *

understood why her brother had loved Madison so. She was everyone's safe place.

Drunk-Dialing

The salty ocean air smelled more imposing, almost worming its way through the cracks in the old beach house. Rory had left

Madison's with a bottle of expensive wine that Hannah's dark-eyed protector had insisted she take home. The bottle sat on the bar, uncorked and almost empty, the smell blending sweetly with the salty ocean. Rory was snoring on the makeshift couch when her phone rung beside her.

"Hey, sweetie…." Rory composed herself for Will, her head hazy.

"What are you doing?" Rory squinted at the phone's vague illumination through the blackness, confirming Will's number.

● ● ●

"Sleeping...it's late...." Her haze didn't cloud this caller's fishiness.

"What are *you* wearing??" Rory sat up abruptly.

"Holden...is that you?!" William never called her late.

"Talk, say anything...I just want to hear your voice." Holden slurred his verbs slightly, giving away the secret to his newfound confidence.

"Why are you calling me from William's phone?" Panic emanated from her dry throat.

"I knew you'd answer if *he* called. I wasn't so sure you'd pick up if it were me." Holden sighed with alcohol-induced self-pity.

"You're a little drunk, aren't you?" Rory giggled, oddly amused.

• • •

"If you don't want to talk to me, then just hang up." Holden morphed into a whiny version of his insecurities.

"Of course I want to talk to you... but....only drunk people call and talk to each other at 2 a.m." Rory fell back onto the mattress, giggling uncontrollably. Holden could hear the liquor on her tongue now.

"Christ Rory!" Holden watched the ice melt, shifting the diluted remnants in his glass.

"Don't get all defensive...You *did* just drunk dial Will's mother from *his* phone and start asking her *tawdry* questions...." Rory smiled at the silhouette of the wine bottle on the counter, smelling its oaky vapors bounce off the receiver as she spoke.

"Tawdry...who in the hell says *tawdry*??" Holden tossed a crumpled paper ball up into the air, catching it repeatedly.

● ● ●

142

The alcohol had restored some commonality. She wondered if their solidarity would now volley.

"How's Will?" Rory ran her fingers through her mop of hair as if he could see her through the phone.

"Will's more than alright...he's perfect..." Silence followed his admonitions once too prideful to reveal.

"...He does piss me off. He's so damn logical and bullheaded...so hard on me." Holden crumpled the paper ball tighter.

"He is *very* protective of his mother...but he's loyal... just like you." Anticipation twisted in their breathing.

"At least I gave you the best of me and, oh, how I'd love to give it to you again." Rory squealed at Holden's sexy insinuation. They tossed the love that remained easily and with folly.

● ● ●

"I'm wearing your old faded blue polo shirt." Rory picked at the top button of the threadbare polo shirt wondering what their life could be like together now.

"Our kid's asleep, so you can talk as dirty to his daddy as you'd like." Rory liked their pretending. She knew Holden had been mourning the lost years with Will.

"Rory, I'm so homesick for you." Holden threw the paper ball into the trashcan. He began yawning, giving in to the alcohol's lullaby.

"I've been homesick, too." Rory played with the ruby ring that once again hung around her neck.

"I miss this…this thing we do…go back and forth. Well, I didn't mean it like that…it just keeps coming…." Holden groaned.

"I think you need to shut up now." Rory snickered at his string of double innuendos.

● ● ●

"Tell me the story. What have you been doing?" Rory's eyes roamed the warm rusty walls.

"I've been painting the place, cleaning the house up. It's coming into itself. *A blank canvas begging for color* Gabby would say."

"What color?"

"You'll just have to come see for yourself." Rory rolled the ruby ring on her pinkie. She had skillfully crafted her invitation.

"I'll be there in two weeks." Holden yawned.

Rory cried through her wide smile.

Strange Transmissions

Rory straightened Gabby's painting. She was always dumbfounded by Gabby's seemingly

● ● ●

effortless use of color and style, a natural extension of her hand connected to her soul. She studied the erratic brushstrokes, finding that Gabby's energy resonated off every canvas she had painted in her short existence. A serene scenic landscape or a vivid sunset all had hints of subtle motion as if they were alive and busy. Gabby's painting seemed to energize the old house's makeover. Rory had dipped into her savings to buy a few furniture pieces for the living room and a few necessities missing from the kitchen. The clutter was gone. Gabby's room remained untouched. It was its own masterpiece, needing nothing. The old beach house had new vigor. Rory had given it all her energy, clearing out the uncomfortable bits of its history.

Madison had arrived to take Rory to the local art gallery. Rory gawked awkwardly at the canvas, lost in other days, as Madison lightly

• • •

rapped on the open door. Madison was counselor and omniscient observer of all things. She didn't speak, looking on with a compassionate smile, astutely aware of Rory's nonverbal inquisition of the painter.

"You ready…are you OK?" Rory's profile was peaked and pale.

"Yeah…I'm just a little off today." Rory brooded, stalling Madison's invitation. "You look more than off. You look a bit green…." Madison closed the door.

"I just miss them." Rory voice was soft and somber.

"Holden is still coming, isn't he?"

"Yes." Angst was stamped on Rory's brow.

"AND this is *good*, isn't it?" Madison was having trouble adding up Rory's odd, weepy despondence. Madison noticed Rory's face was

* * *

puffy and there were visible dark circles under her eyes, shrieking lack of sleep.

"Will's staying in Breckenridge." Rory squinted at the painting, almost angry in her sadness and scrutiny; its brush strokes now mocked her son's absence. Rory navigated from tearful to irate in mere seconds. Her loneliness was gift wrapped in anger. Her fear rooted her from lack of control.

"Rory, what do *you* want...right now?" Madison pushed past Rory's volatility.

"I just, I just need to get out of my own head... I need to go to that damn art gallery!"

Madison laughed out loud at the eerie similarities between brother and sister. Stalling was their learned behavior as children.

"Then, let's get you the hell out of here!" Madison grabbed Rory's wrist and yanked her toward the door.

* * *

"You know my brother was crazy. It could be genetic." Directness had worked when Rhett stewed with fear or indecision. Rory smiled at Madison, and for an instant, they were really family.

The Gallery

The Grace Christy Alexander gallery was a well-rooted, older structure with petite, narrow architecture. Touristy sky scrapers had sprouted all around it on the Gulf Shores/Pensacola shoreline, giving away the building's age, yet making it a beautiful anomaly. There were lots of tall windows and skylights that suggested it had been another sort of business before it was an art gallery. The structure's proximity was two hundred yards from the beach, letting the windows and skylights dress the showrooms with sand, water, and sunlight.

* * *

Madison opened the tall, steel door to the gallery for Rory, who sighed heavily, pausing before entering. Rory had been silent most of the fifteen minute drive. The displays were partitioned, featuring each artist. There was also a wall of permanent art donated by the artist or purchased by the gallery. Most artists were local or had some ties to the Gulf Coast. The back room of the gallery was Grace Alexander's studio. It provided a glassed-in view as she painted; her art was scattered around the space, her own showing. It was art in motion for those who happened to be touring the displays. Madison knew Grace, a woman in her midforties with thick, curly red hair. She was unmistakable, moving around the studio, preparing to paint a canvas. A young woman greeted them and showed them a list of artists currently on display. Before ushering them into the studio, she conveniently reiterated that she handled the purchase of any paintings of interest.

• • •

"How do people come up with this?" Rory marveled at the first row of paintings. They were sunset beach abstracts that used colors in a washed fashion as if viewing them through a filter.

"Artists just feel differently than the rest of us, I guess." Madison quickly lowered her voice that bounced garishly off the hardwood floors and into the skylights.

"I don't know about that... I've been doing *too* much feeling lately...more than I have in a long, long time." Rory talked over her shoulder towards Madison, her lips contorted weirdly. She gravitated toward an abstract painting consisting of half a dozen wine bottles in deep burgundy accented with a white, thick brush stroke steeped with vibration, giving the viewer a sense of double vision.

"Peacocks keep their baggage closed...and that can be a *bad* thing." Madison slowed, hovering over ... a muted orange

151

sunset painting of a boy flying a kite. The kite was a vibrant purple.

"My bags have been unpacked for a while...Holden is coming for me...Will is starting his life...and..." Madison watched Rory study the painting with frustration and panic. "AND...why does this upset you? It is what you wanted, isn't it?" Faintly, in the corner of one of the bottles, Rory noticed what looked to be a rolled up piece of paper, a message in the bottle?

"*Things* have...well, changed...wait - this...it has to be the same artist that did your painting...." Rory obliviously jumped subjects.

"Now why would you say that?" Madison was growing weary of being evasive.

"Because of the brushstrokes...they are harsh and the color is bold...." Rory squinted, moving very close to the canvas.

"Rory, I'm not talking about the damn painting! What *things* have *changed* other than

* * *

your moods?" Rory's immediacy to the canvas caught the eye of the young concierge. Madison grabbed a chunk of Rory's hair, pulling her away from the painting a bit.

"Quit counseling me!" Rory slapped Madison's hand, turning and running around the corner like a loose child. Everyone in earshot turned to their blaring voices.

Rory rounded the corner and almost crashed into a large canvas that encompassed most of the space. It was a close focused abstract of a small child's fingers fishing for a ground worm deep in a tiny hole in the dirt, using merely a bristle from a broom. It was a game Rory, Holden, and Gabby had played as youth, many southern children practiced it. In most instances, the worm won, but it entertained restless kids for hours. However, this canvas had a palpable ire. It was soft and sentimental in its browns, yet sorrowful, almost bitter with sickly yellow greens mixed with the deeper pines. Grief

● ● ●

seemed to shadow and veil a once pleasant memory.

"Oh, SHIT!" Rory exclaimed inappropriately and even Grace behind the glass turned her head to Rory as if she had shouted it in church with the amen's.

"I think we need to leave, Rory..." Madison moved close to Rory putting her hand on Rory's shoulder. Rory flinched, wiggling away from Madison's rationality.

"I want *this* painting...I'm not leaving until I find out who painted it!" Rory waved at the young woman who scurried to Rory's petulant command.

"The artist goes by BRIE, but I am afraid she isn't selling this one, Ma'am. I'm sorry." The young woman, once so kind, now appeared miffed and flustered.

"Of course you won't sell it to *me*! Who would sell anything to a woman acting like a

● ● ●

154

witch?" Rory ran out of the gallery, slamming the heavy steel door. The thunderous vibrations shifted all the paintings in the first display slightly off their center.

Madison apologized to Grace and the young concierge, giving them a card in case the artist changed her mind about selling the painting. When Madison exited the gallery, she feared Rory had fled on foot until she heard Rory morosely throwing her guts up on a beautifully ornate palm tree. Madison grabbed Rory's hair once again, this time to hold it out of her face as she vomited. She steadied Rory, rubbing her back.

The two women got into the car, both red faced and silent.

"I'm pregnant." Rory began sobbing. Madison started the car.

"Thank God. I thought you *were* crazy like your brother." Madison pulled Rory into her

• • •

arms. "Witchy Woman" by the Eagles played softly on the radio as the two alternated laughter with tears.

Madison made a few phone calls to her children before driving Rory back to the beach house. She barked out ultimatums for her son to her take-charge daughter. Rory could tell Madison's love originated in her finesse, the reassuring structure she provided in her children's lives. The drive back to the house was as somber and heavy as before. Not a word was spoken. When Rory sniveled tears like freak rain showers, Madison reached for her hand in consolation, shushing Rory's sobs like she would her own toddler. The eerie silence provided shelter.

Walking through the beach house door mirrored returning to a murder scene. Madison glanced at the painting of Gabby's above the couch, the reds and bold colors bleeding emotions all over the room. Rory opened the

• • •

156

refrigerator, offering Madison something to drink. She poured them both a ginger ale over ice, hoping to soothe her queasiness. They sat on the new couch, listening to the ginger ale's bubbles fizz, cracking the ice in their glasses.

"So, are you *sure* you are pregnant?"

Rory started to tune up again, pointing to the bathroom. Madison followed her finger, flipping on the light switch to find six pregnancy test boxes tossed wildly, one soggy in the toilet. Lined up neatly on the counter were six white tester sticks revealing a plus sign on *every* one.

"Is the baby Holden's?" Madison crossed her arms in a sisterly fashion, goading past Rory's sullen tears.

"Yes, it is Holden's baby!" Rory threw her snotty tissue in Madison's direction.

"So why isn't this good news? Why can't you feel the joy?" Madison sat by Rory on the couch, reaching for her hand once again.

• • •

"I tried to deny it at first. Then, the nausea hit hard…horrible morning sickness like when I was pregnant with Will…all alone." Rory lowered her head, rubbing the small pone that was already making her pants uncomfortable. "I guess I just wanted my life to be different."

"Maybe this baby is your life. It is the difference. It's just waiting for you." Madison gently touched Rory's stomach.

Madison's phone vibrated from her purse. She reached to answer it, snarling her nose suspiciously at the caller before excusing herself and striding into the bedroom. Rory heard Madison's deep, southern intonation through the paper thin walls, her tenor questioning and surprised.

"You aren't going to believe this… that was the gallery. The artist has agreed to sell you the painting." Madison smiled cautiously.   ● ● ●

"Why would they do *that?*" Rory rubbed her temples, now totally embarrassed at her meltdown.

"I told them I thought you were pregnant…so very pregnant." Madison poured them more ginger ale.

● ● ●

September 2010

Seeds

Madison took Rory to her gynecologist. The doctor was a very personable, middleaged lady with short silver hair and a dimpled smile. She confirmed Rory's pregnancy, estimating she was about nine weeks along. Rory wept in chance waves, denying the delightful news. The doctor was savvy, noticing Rory's diffidence. She had discovered it to be a typical reaction for women over forty who discover they are pregnant. She encouraged Rory to connect with her untapped emotions regarding the baby. But, Rory was determined not to disturb the beehive that buzzed with fury, coursing a motherly madness through her veins. At least not until Holden knew. Rory hadn't told the doctor that twenty years prior she had denied her son's existence for the sake

* * *

of her sanity. Joy finally rose the day William pushed from her body.

Holden would be arriving for lunch. The beach house was in a manageable order thanks to Madison's help. She had given Rory a few pieces of furniture. A dining room table that she now had set for two and small pieces that made the space officially new and livable. Rory held her breath while preparing their seafood salad sandwiches. The seafood's strong odor sent a wave of nausea over her. The ginger ale offered little comfort.

The gallery had delivered the ground worm painting days earlier. It was a thick framed canvas that was 40x40, engulfing the khaki wall where Rory hung it. Rory had scrutinized the painting style as she tried to match it with Gabby's twenty-year-old canvas. She rolled Holden's ruby ring nervously around her finger. The differences outweighed the similarities. Seems BRIE's art was unafraid

● ● ●

and unforgiving of any use of color or style –
Gabby times four. She truly blended the joys
with the tragedies of her life, swirling them into
a concrete, relatable tapestry. Rory scanned the
room and sighed deeply. Children shrieked in
high-pitched bursts as they raced in the sand.
She held her breath again, this time taking in
the new seeds in her life that she and Holden
had scattered rather unconsciously. In
maternal fashion, Rory purposefully caressed
the promise and innocence that now grew
inside her.

Everything Old

Holden knocked on the old wooden door with
three familiar taps. As far back as Rory could
remember, when their longing was new and
uncharted, his fists had bled urgency and
desire. Rory turned the new doorknob she had

● ● ●

installed, opening the door into a sea of red petals. The man that peered around the roses startled Rory at first. Holden's Cheshire smile was salt and pepper. He had grown a goatee and lost weight. He was wearing penny loafers and an old, worn navy blazer over his crisp white shirt, and his hair was shorter, allowing the fine creases in his brow to show his age. Combined with his glasses, he now epitomized boyish charm. His eyes traveled Rory's body, starting at her feet. She was wearing a dress again. This one was flowing with black with white polka dots, contouring her ample hips and derriere.

Rory's chestnut hair was shorter and Holden could see the way her neck rose delicately from her strong shoulders. He handed her the roses with fragile care as he walked through the doorway.

Rory searched for a makeshift vase,

* * *

finding an old water carafe that did the trick. Her eyes combed the corners, panicked when she didn't see his luggage. Holden stood with his hands in his jean pockets, observing her every sway with methodical silence. As Rory proudly placed the roses on the dining room table, Holden reached from behind her, wrapping his long forearm around her waist and stomach. She turned into him quickly and they stood nose to nose. They postured as old lovers, intrinsically familiar with each other. She tickled his goatee with her nosy fingertips. His hand roved her hip as he grunted in some man language.

"I'd better go get my luggage from the car." He squeezed her buttock with his long fingers, brushing his new whiskers across her cheek bone.

"I have always liked you in glasses." Rory ran her quick fingers through his hair, straightening his ... shirt collar, resting her hand affectionately on his jaw line. Holden watched the panic retreat into the corners of her almond-shaped green eyes. Everything old was now something new, something more.

Rory served their sandwiches with nervous attention, hearing the slam of Holden's trunk. His shadow moved through the blinds and along the walls of the beach house. The vocal wheels on his large suitcase squealed in agony. Rory pretended to arrange the flowers in the vase, watching him awkwardly maneuver the fossil over the door footing as if it were loaded with cinderblocks. He pronounced it dead, throwing his blazer over the well worn handle. It was then that Holden began to focus on more than just the chemistry in the room. The old walls were warm and the details and precision of Rory's renovation left him mute. They sat at the old mahogany table once Madison's from her previous life with Rhett. The chairs were

● ● ●

overstuffed and comfortable, almost as if they'd never been used.

"You really worked hard on this old house." Holden looked to the once ransacked kitchen, finding order; canisters that once held junk now sat on the countertop with flour and sugar. A knife set and a complete set of utensils for cooking were close to the stove top.

"She has a lot promise and history…too much life left in her to just… give up." Rory picked at her sandwich, nauseated. The seafood salad had grown more pungent closed up in its container.

"I can't wait to see and hear about…everything." Holden devoured his sandwich in calculated gulps, reaching for her plate where he thieved her uneaten bites.

"So, larceny *is* genetic…you men…you steal a lady's uneaten food…and somehow that is

* * *

supposed to be smooth?" Rory plucked a rose from the vase, swatting his guilty fingers.

Holden relinquished her sandwich with a toothy smile. He kissed her fingertips and she tossed the sandwich back onto his plate. He devoured it.

"I noticed there are twenty roses." She strategically placed the rose back in the vase. Holden took their empty plates to the sink.

"One for every year I missed…every Valentine's Day…and Will's birthday." Car doors slammed in mismatched harmony as a new family descended next door. Their pitched chatter bounced between the houses, laced with excitement and anticipation.

Rory cleared the remaining dishes, joining Holden at the sink. There was no dishwasher. Holden washed the dishes in a sink of sudsy hot water just as he had many Vansant summers

* * *

ago. Rory rinsed them before drying them, stacking them neatly on the counter.

"How's William?" Rory's green eyes softened in the creases.

"He's good. We are still getting to know each other." Holden wiped away the last bits of seafood salad from a plate, their shoulders inches apart.

"What have you learned?" Rory dried a cup repeatedly.

"He likes photography and journalism…and red-headed women." Rory bumped shoulders with Holden knocking him off balance.

"He's a good man that loves and respects his very strong mother… almost as much as I do." Holden looked to Rory, his eyes begging forgiveness. Rory passed Holden a tender kiss on the lips.

* * *

"Has Will found a school?" Rory positioned the plates on top of the others that were stacked neatly with precision just as she had her motherly inquisition.

"I think he is looking at a school in Denver." Everything seemed to have a place, mismatched or not. Holden searched the very well-organized cabinets, combing for the glasses' proper rest.

"He was…sidetracked…when he found out there was a chance we could get back together…he needs to go back... finish what he started." Holden read into Rory's cryptic theme, slipping his fingers over hers as he guided her to the couch.

"Will really didn't have choices…but now…he has the world." Holden looked at Rory's renovation with fresh vision, seeing behind the neat rows and perfect placement. Motherhood was one of her beautiful strengths.

● ● ●

"Will is a finisher. He is a lot like you, here. He knows how to fill his time productively. He has been my handyman." They sat side by side on the couch, holding hands like teenagers.

Thunder rumbled in the distance as the sky flickered through the racing clouds in sonic bursts of light and dark.

"When you've lived in a cage, you learn to adapt it to your comfort. I just don't want him to find that comfort confining." Rory ran her fingertip in circles over the callused palm of his hand.

Holden looked at the abstract art she had strategically placed on the walls. He recognized the one painting as Gabby's. It was signed with a flamboyant G.

"Tell me the story of that worm hole canvas. Where did you find it?" His eyes fixated on the oddly moody painting. He was

• • •

stunned at the detailed sadness painted in this forsaken, fond memory.

"I bought it at a local gallery…I remember when all three of us were kids fishing those damn things out for hours…it called me…I'd swear it was Gabby's."
Holden looked from one painting to the other, comparing styles.

"I think Gabby would be honored to have her art hang on a nail." The wind gusts peppered the windowpanes with rain that demanded their attention.

Holden and Rory directed their concentration to the window as the gale imposed itself ruthlessly. Harmless objects now took on brutal force. Plastic beach chairs scuttled across the deck and into the door and windows. Metal wind chimes that sang sweetly became shrill, sharp weapons that beat the window pane angrily. Quick, violent bursts

• • •

of rain deluged the beach house in whining, mismatched waves. Just as quickly as the storm swelled, it retreated with the tides, leaving low, gray clouds that hovered like monsters, combing the beach for the innocent and unaware. The whining winds died abruptly to still. The power surged like a wounded dinosaur before finally going out. Their ears had not yet adjusted when they heard the old floorboard creek in Gabby's room. They remained statuesque, listening to the white noise of adrenaline rushing their brains.

"I think this place is haunted. I've heard a lot of bumps in the night since I've been here alone." Holden felt Rory's grip grow goliath and firm.

"I think we're the ones haunted." Holden was aware of heaviness, an energy he didn't recognize in the room.

• • •

"Let's get out of here." Rory was green and pale. Holden stood, his fingers still laced in hers. He watched her with concern as she ambled to the door.

The deck was littered with debris from distant neighbors. The beach was dark, a ghost town for as far as the eye could see. They shed their shoes on the steps and walked in the cool, damp sand. Holden could see Rory's color returning after watching her fight back against something he didn't understand. The wind blew a cool, less humid breeze that seemed to restore their stability. They walked to the water's edge arm in arm, admiring the crystal clarity in the landscape the storm had left behind. Their vision was crisper and less opaque. Other beach goers began appearing from their powerless abodes, walking the beach as well, searching for light and energy.

"Remember the first time we ever came here with the Vansants? The power went out

● ● ●

overnight and we had to sleep with our windows open." Everyone moved like the undead, mumbling at the tides in a low, groveling chatter.

"Yeah, I remember the teenagers on the beach, listening to music and talking late into the night." Holden had fallen asleep to the tempo of their voices.

"Talking has quickly become a forgotten art." Rory's neck flushed with agitation as she watched kids with their cell phones frantically texting the power outage news to their friends. Holden got the impression that Rory had pulled at Will's shirt collar thousands of times in reprimand.

The gray afternoon hung in shadows of sporadic sunlight until the surge of electricity coursed through the beach houses with an audible pop. The houses radiated a prism of color throughout the mass of newly lit windows. Holden ... and Rory turned their eyes to their old house just as the power returned.

In the window to Gabby's loft, a shadowy figure seemed hung as mist, clingy and elusive as fog. It stood motionless, teasing the duo that held hands in solidarity. Rory felt a wave of nausea she couldn't deny. She fell to her knees, spewing seafood salad on the sand. Holden dueled with his instincts, choosing Rory over the intruder. He knelt beside her, rubbing her back.

"What the hell are you doing, Holden?!" Rory wretched again and Holden jumped up in disgust and confusion.

"Christ, Rory, you are obviously sick." Holden tried to help her stand, but she barfed on his bare feet and he danced in the pink conglomeration as if navigating hot coals.

"I'm fine...Go...check the house...." Rory groaned, falling into her own strewn

• • •

vomit. Holden looked to the upstairs window, but the mist had mysteriously vanished.

Holden scooped Rory into his stature and calmly walked her back to the house as onlookers gawked morbidly. The kids on their cell phones tapped away in mute mockery. He got her safely inside, closing the blinds before unzipping her dress. She willingly peeled out of the vomit stained mess. He laid Rory on the couch, covering her with the old blazer he had thrown on his forgotten suitcase.

Holden crept up the creaky stairs to find the door to Gabby's room bolted securely with the master lock Rory had installed. He reached above the door frame and found the key, unlocking it. A small decorative stained glass window that was high near the peak of the roof had blown out, shattering colorful shards across Gabby's floor. The storm's forceful winds blew through the broken window, manipulating Gabby's mannequin. It had fallen

● ● ●

forward into the window's view before crashing to the floor. Holden footed the mannequin before picking it up, placing the wig back on its bald head. He kicked the shards of glass into one corner of the room, casing for signs of foul play before locking the door.

Holden studied Rory from the top of the stairs. Rory's red underwear was sexy under his navy blazer that she was now wearing. She was sitting up now as she reached for her glass of ginger ale, wincing as she brought it to her nose. She sat the glass down, throwing her head back, moaning in an odd disgust. He descended the stairs slowly.

"The wind blew out that small window upstairs...Gabby's mannequin was the intruder. You OK?" Holden stood beside her, his hands in his pockets.

"You remind me of William standing

● ● ●

there like that. He is my helpless hover bug."
Rory smiled through her squeamishness.

Holden bent down, kissing her on the
cheek. He joined her on the couch, pulling her
into him, his long body cocooning her safely.
The refrigerator hummed sporadically like an
old noisy cricket never freed, tethered to the
house's old ghosts. Within minutes, Rory was
snoring. Holden held her, searching the corners
of her mouth for the things she hadn't spoken
that afternoon.

Pregnant Pauses

Holden lie wrapped around Rory, listening to
her metered breathing, imagining the dreams
that bounced around her brain as she twitched
from time to time.

"How long have I napped?" Rory yawned,
muffling the last ... part of her sentence

with her cupped hand. Holden kissed her cheek and she snuggled back into him. The storm and the power surge seemed a distant memory.

"A couple of hours I think." Holden had been awake for half an hour, staring at his suitcase. He had purposely left it by the door just in case. He presumed nothing after their last tango of words. They lie still for a long while, absorbing the fluency of their bodies.
"So…what's your life like in

Breckenridge…at Gabby's?" Rory's syllables were garbled, hushed.

"Atypical. The town is cozy with young and old moving everywhere." The sun's lower, orange trajectory now blinded them through the open shades.

"I bet William loves the rush of crowds...makes him feel connected to the pulse of people again." Rory remembered their closed off life under Rhett's scrutiny.

● ● ●

"I live above the restaurant and bar. It can get nuts and isolating at times. People can rage in crowds as easily as cheer and I live on top of it." Rory imagined his man cave, sparse in browns and blues.

"You get lonely in crowds, don't you?" Rory wiggled loose, needing to validate that Holden's eyes and face matched his tone. "...and you don't, do you? You and Will are people watchers. You don't have to engage in conversation to connect." Holden tried to rub away the zigzagged creases his shirt had pressed in her puffy cheeks.

"But you...Holden Hitchfield...you love to stir the pot...you like to see what's floating in the soup." Holden eyed her creamy flesh that protruded in glints with her movement.

"Rory, owning a bar is like being a preacher. You've got a congregation whose

* * *

vices match their virtues, but in the end, they are all come together for the same reasons."

Holden watched Rory tug at the old navy blazer, working to hide herself deep inside its lining.

"I think I'm going to change…or maybe just put some clothes on again." Holden watched her walk to the bedroom, pulling something to wear from the closet before slipping into the bathroom. She flung his navy blazer out the door in his direction.

Holden moved to the bedroom, retrieving his jacket off the floor. He breathed in the lining, taking in Rory's skin. Drawers and cabinets slammed as she fumbled with what he imagined was woman voodoo, magic potions that rendered him ineffective.

Holden cased Rory's nightstand as she mixed her potions in various clinks and clanks that emanated behind the bathroom door. He

● ● ●

found a picture of Will as a toddler. He coveted Will's chubby cheeks and jolly smile, wondering if Will had yet to figure out his father's absence. He tucked his hands in his pockets with a sigh, pivoting abruptly before leaving the room.

Holden liked the rusty red living room walls. Rory had said they made the borders of the room stand out, particularly the worm hole painting. It dominated his periphery like a stop sign. Holden was compelled to touch its hilly paint, running his fingers over the textured surfaces. It felt akin to Gabby's work. Rory had placed it in the center of the room and it seemed to feed on the unsuspecting who dared to give it attention.

He looked at Gabby's painting off in an obscure corner. Time had compromised the old acrylic paint. Its bold reds had faded. Its brittle texture was losing its initial edginess. Oddly, Holden felt a rush of sadness. The knot in his

● ● ●

throat that surrounded this tragedy began swelling with grave sharpness. He felt that heavy, guilty energy in the house again; the heaviness of the old ghosts that seemed to be pushing him and Rory together, forward with its powerful historical momentum.

Rory's shorts were getting snug. She hadn't dare changed clothes in front of him fearing he'd notice her fattening midsection that was constricted even with the elastic waistband. She was practicing how she'd tell Holden about the baby when she heard the ceiling boards creak and pop. She had slept below Gabby in this room all those summers ago and could always tell when Gabby was on the move. No matter how graceful, Gabby's boards never lied. Nausea's anxiety rushed Rory as she strained her ears for more signs of activity. There was nothing, but Rory swore she could feel another heart beating amidst the humidity.

● ● ●

Holden had heard the creaking, was looking up at the locked room when Rory ambushed him with the tenacity of the tides, washing into him and delicately ransacking his personal space. The hair on her arms was now standing on end. They stood still, their dog-like wits keen, searching for sounds or smells they wouldn't acknowledge verbally, smirking in anticipation at the worm hole painting as if waiting for it to confess its truths. Holden broke forward, removing the canvas, pulling it down from its astute prerogative. He demoted it to the corner, replacing it with Gabby's fading masterpiece, emboldened with a large G.

"That's much better...you ready to go eat?" Holden adjusted his thick-framed glasses in approval, digging his pockets for the keys to his car as he marched to the door.

"Actually, I'm starving." As Rory turned the lock on the knob, she looked through the window pane at the painting now sitting

• • •

powerlessly in the corner. The hair on the back of her neck stood on end in rippling waves. Holden offered Rory his arm and they sealed their alliance, pushing their thread effortlessly through the eye of the needle.

The Old Haunt

There was a little seafood restaurant just down from the small marina where John Vansant had kept his boat docked bayside. Holden drove them back to the scene of the crime as he had promised her in their phone conversation before he returned to the beach. The parking lot was gravel and the old grocery store still had an eighties gas pump. The building was weathered operating as a convenience store and bait shop. Holden noticed the phone booth where he had made a call that June night, the phone gone to technology. They passed the wooden marina

● ● ●

that had been neglected, patched in places with few ships docked. John Vansant's end space was abandoned, the boards rotted around the footing. Rory's eyes hung onto the marina as they moved past to the restaurant that sat right on the bay.

The restaurant was all wooden inside and out, intended to make the customer feel a part of the scene as if they had just stepped off their boat. It might have been effective at one time, but it just seemed more caricature than ambiance. They sat in a quiet corner with a bay view of the ships coming in and out. Steaming plates passed by with the waitress on a huge platter, enticing their noses. Their waitress finally approached their table, breaking their indifference as they fumbled with the menu, searching for a dinner choice. Holden ordered a beer and fried shrimp and Rory a catfish Po-boy with extra sweet pickles and spicy horseradish. The pair watched other diners,

• • •

finding strangers' lives more relevant than their own in this old, tricky haunt.

Holden held Rory's hand, working to sew the ripped fabric of their past with reverent temperance. When their dinner arrived, it was heaping portions fit for a sailor and his crew. Holden polished off his second beer, watching Rory load her Po-boy. She smeared the horseradish and extra sweet pickles all over her sandwich. He scowled sarcastically, putting his ear to her plate to see if the fish filet was screaming for mercy. Rory dug into her messy sandwich with a fork and Holden belly laughed at her sudden case of manners. He picked up his jumbo shrimp with his fingers in mockery of her fork, dipping it in the cocktail sauce and then into the vat of horseradish she hoarded. She jabbed at his fingers and he retracted them, sucking the stolen sauce from his fingernail. Rory picked up the large sandwich and loaded her small mouth with a gigantic bite.

• • •

Horseradish and sweet pickles oozed out like volcanic lava. Holden scooped up the sandwich drippings with his shrimp, tasting it and giving her an audible grunt of approval. It was only then that Rory noticed that their unintended foreplay had garnered an audience. An older couple was sitting cattycornered, watching their performance. They abruptly reeled in their display. Holden began using his fork, wiping the excess sauce out of the corner of Rory's mouth with his napkin. The couple finished up their wine and got up to leave when the gentleman gave them a surprising thumbs up before taking his ticket to the cashier. The lady stranger had short salt and pepper hair, reminiscent of Lexie. She walked past their table, winking affectionately. Holden ordered another beer.

Rory ordered dessert.

The sun was falling behind distant billowed clouds. Holden went to pay for

● ● ●

dinner, watching as Rory rummaged through a basket of mints. The cashier informed them that the older couple that was seated nearby had paid for their dinner. He handed them a note written on the back of their ticket obviously signed by the lady who had beautiful cursive. It read: *Go for it.* Holden shared the note with Rory who just stared at it with a smitten grin. Holden folded it carefully and placed it in his wallet behind the keepsake picture of Rory.

They pushed open the over-sized wooden door and their flip flops popped as loudly as the old wooden boardwalk. The place had become a ghost town with sunset. Only remnants of people remained as seagulls bobbed over a spilled container of popcorn. Rory handed Holden a toothpick and they picked their teeth in distraction as they neared the marina. The partly cloudy sky cast shades of gray and purple across the old wood and metal harbor. They held hands, peering at the empty marina

• • •

that once housed the Vansant's boat, the very dock where Gabby had died. The sun gilded their faces, highlighting the whites of their eyes.

"It doesn't hurt the same, does it?" Rory flicked her toothpick into the bay. It bobbed like a buoy.

"No, it's just closure now...loose ends." Holden threw his toothpick beside hers and a wave sent the pair of sticks floating off together under the dock.

"I want this to be closure...that our life will be some semblance of normal...but I don't think it exists with us...and I'm OK with it." Rory crossed her arms in self-assurance.

"I don't believe in *normal* when it comes to you and me." Holden had his hands in his pockets, jiggling his loose change.

● ● ●

"There's never been anything normal about us – ever." Rory kicked at the loose boards, testing their fragility.

"Frankly, I've learned to like living with the devil in the details…living for us, *now*." Holden leaned into her, wrapping his long arms around her. They watched the sun finally succumb to the night.

"*Now* feels so good, Holden…are you sure it isn't a sin?" Holden pulled Rory into him, kissing her, tasting the horseradish on her tongue.

"Let me take you back to the beach house and show you what a sin is." Seagulls swooped in on the breath of their energy.

"Holden…" Rory grinned mischievously out of the corner of her mouth. "…I'm pregnant."

Holden froze at first. He jumped backwards,   ● ● ●   examining Rory with a gawk of utter panic. He began to connect the dots to her recurring reticence.

"I've been trying to tell you…but that lady's note…." Rory put her trembling hand on her round stomach. Holden watched her simple, motherly gesture, his eyes wild with questions.

"Christ Rory…how…but I…" His nightfallen shadow paced in circles, buzzing like a fly to a lamp light. The old plank under his footing couldn't take his frenzy. It gave way, dumping Holden into the murky bay.

It was an eternal second before Holden surfaced. When he did, he began whooping and hollering as he treaded water, his new glasses crooked on his forehead. His grin grew wide with elation. Rory jumped into the salty water, clinging to him, kissing him over and over.

* * *

Spirit Flesh

Their dank clothes had soaked the rental car and permeated the beach house with dirty, fishy odors. Holden shed his shirt as he locked the deadbolt. Rory ran her hands along the walls and furniture, finding it ironic that they were sneaking back into this house they had snuck out of so many times to make love on John's boat. Rory fingered her way into the bedroom with Holden hot on her heels, his breaths synced with her own. He ran his hand over her hip grunting in his man language while she searched for the bathroom light switch. Its illumination had always been diffuse and intimate, softening their facial features. They studied each other for those old cues, finding their old habits invigorating once again.

Rory unbuttoned Holden's shorts. She pulled them south, ... revealing his navy pinstriped boxers. His long legs were comical, skinnier and hairier than she remembered. Holden pulled her t-shirt off over her head, locking her arms overhead as he kissed her breasts that now hung appealingly lower with ripening pregnancy fruits. He affectionately kissed her cleavage before moving to her swollen belly. Their sweet, spicy skin mingled with traces of rotting sea life. He moved his lips in smitten circles around her belly button and Rory twirled the graying hair on his crown, finding the swirls of white and silver unusually sexy. Holden reached into the shower and spun the knob 180 degrees. They were half-naked, half-clothed when the steam began to fill up the room and they pawed at the others' pink figure that was losing physical form, morphing into globs of spirit flesh. Rory's giggles echoed off the old tile shower as they disappeared into the fog, melding with the steamy walls.

● ● ●

"I've always been in love with you...." The soap and lotion had followed them to the bed. Holden murmured gently into her damp ear, running his long fingers over her stomach.

"I know." Rory snickered and Holden's meandering fingers gripped her side with firm tickles. He noticed they had showered long enough to wrinkle their skin like raisins.

"Christ, Rory...look at *us*." He pinned her shoulders down with the sheet, and he began kissing her neck as she squirmed, finally wooed by his new whiskers.

"I *know*..." Rory rolled him over, straddling his waist. Her potbelly was now her most prominent and beloved feature.

Pregnant pauses highlighted the uncertainty of what was truly happening between them. Repressed fears had fueled a very fickle reunion just a few months earlier. They deliberated their lust with textbook eyes,

● ● ●

futilely searching for the reasons, magic words that described the flutter in their guts.

Rory ran her hands over his fuzzy chest and he caressed her thighs. The unspoken had been crossed as they folded into each other with wicked precision, audibly unapologetic. They fused their bodies into one sinewy monster. Holden had one leg and Rory one arm sticking out from under the covers; appendages with odd machinations, mangled as a pile of hangers.

After they had made love, they muttered low, soft language, staring in unison at the long cracks in the ceiling where the plaster was compromised. It had crumbled, revealing the boards, silently likened to the roadmaps in their past, often convoluted, tedious, and winding. It was only at the cracks' intersection that the two lines ultimately abandoned self-destruction, remarkably shoring up the ceiling's strength in the most unexpected places. The baby that

* * *

bounced around to their shameless syncopation was affirmation of life's mad karmic timing.

Moving On

Holden and Rory fixated on the morning skyline over their steaming coffee cups. Their shoulders touched slightly, making their chemistry electric and fuzzy around the edges. The crescent moon was a mere sliver, a slight opening to heaven that sat quizzically in the dawn's purple horizon. The ocean was flat, meandering casually to the moon's mantra. A dog walked along side its owner, bouncing occasionally in the sand to the innate, quiet reverence of a new day. A new window of time unfolded just as slight as the solar breeze at sunrise.

"You know I used to think we had all this time. I had all these reasons and promises I

● ● ●

couldn't keep to you. Then, in an instant there you were here again and with

Will. I realized it isn't about time anymore." Holden's mind replayed his years of yearning and loneliness as the coffee energized his brain.

"We had made all these plans and after that horrible night on the boat, I had to pick at pieces of you I could find…pieces of you in Will, and here you are again." Rory lined up the crazy symmetry of their parallel lives.

"So, we're on the same blank page?" Holden held his breath.

"To blank pages…" Rory stroked the fuzzy hair on his strong forearms.

"Good. I just want to love you, raise our baby with you." Holden wrapped his arm around Rory's waist watching the moon fade into the blue with sunrise.

● ● ●

"You do realize you are asking me to raise a baby in a bar?" Rory put her head on his shoulder with a shaky sigh.

"I…I guess I am." Holden worried slightly until he heard her giggling grow.

"Good. I would *love* to raise our baby in a bar with you." Rory took Holden's coffee cup and placed it on the boardwalk beside her own. She jumped up and took his hand with childlike enthusiasm, tugging at his strong forearm, ushering him to walk the beach.

They headed west as the sun warmed their backs, lengthening their shadows in front of them. In the sunrise, old voices spoke like the spirits attached to their shared story. Their collective thoughts passed over them in ripples of laughter and tears, freeing them from their illusions, closing the windows to their doubt. They walked hand in hand, passing other sleepy tourists moving like mannequins, slow and drone. The ●●● ritual of praising the new morning was evident in the sounds and smells of coffee and bacon wafting from porches and open windows. The busy world was briefly in sync.

Crystal blue eyes snooped over a newspaper, locking in with a personal fixation that garnered Holden's concentration. Madison watched them pass her boardwalk, her interest banal on the surface, yet intent, almost vested. Madison's eyes had always kept every ones' secrets even before she hid them for a living as a counselor. They were the glints in her pupils, sparkling like trophies on a shelf. Holden had felt her fishing his body language when she exchanged Gabby's journals with Rory back in June. Madison's approach was potent and protective.

"That woman over there...I don't know what to make of her." Holden smiled childishly in Madison's direction while questioning her sincerity.

• • •

"*That* woman is a force. She kept protecting Will and me long after Rhett's death. She didn't have to do that, you know." Rory found herself defending Madison and it felt gratifying to pay her back through the only means she had, her goodwill.

"Her eyes just…linger…and I feel like she knows more. I mean, she was married to your brother." Holden knew Rhett must have married Madison for a good reason. He wasn't in partnerships for love alone. She had to have subtle skills he had exploited.

"Yes, Madison and Rhett were a lot alike. If they loved you, they were loyal. They got the job done. She took good care of William…and she knows about our baby. She's got our back." Rory leered snidely and Holden knew he didn't want to know some facets of Rory's past life in a cage run by the Peacocks.

● ● ●

"I like thinking she has *yours*." Holden kissed Rory's fingertips blatantly as Madison's eyes fell behind her newspaper once again, covering a grin they couldn't fathom.

Bottle it Up

A freak September shower had drained their drive. They were awake and aware, listening to the sounds of the old house as it creaked and settled with the bursts of wind, mangled snuggly in their bed linens, still not ready to face the cloudy morning's chore of packing up the beach house. Rory closed her eyes and could almost hear Gabby stomping across the floor in her room above. She would rap several times, letting Rory know she was awake. Holden felt Rory wiggle lose, readjusting her pot belly that seemed to get in the way of her usual resting position almost

• • •

overnight. He remembered the times that he had snuck into this bedroom after the Vansants had polished off three bottles of wine, their buzzed ears mute to teenage lusty footsteps. Now, he's making love to her in the same room that felt like the birthplace of his libido and their infatuation.

Holden's eyes cased the room. He liked the warm paint colors Rory had chosen. They were clean, accenting the small, colorful trinkets she had symmetrically placed in corners, walls, and dressers. His eyes lingered, combed an odd glass bottle that sat on the dresser with some rolled-up note paper.

"What's in that bottle?" Holden pointed his big toe attached to a very long leg in the direction of the dresser.

"It's something I found when cleaning up. It was a peculiar note of Gabby's. It is written on some strange watermarked paper or something. I don't ••• know…I couldn't throw it away." Rory pulled away from Holden, her body comfortably naked now, wearing only her panties around him. He watched her fish the paper from the bottle, tossing it on the bed. Holden examined it, holding the watermark to the light. It looked like a chemist's artwork.

Rory delicately rolled it, securing it with a paperclip before putting it back in the bottle. It was unique art indeed.

"How do we bottle this place up, Rory?" Holden wrapped his arms and legs around Rory, pulling her back into bed.

"The only good crap worth taking is Gabby's. The rest is just crap." Rory rolled on top of Holden and the old, bowl shaped bed squeaked loudly. She bounced up and down, giggling at the vocal ancient springs. "You are right, just a bunch of old crap." Holden and Rory had tested the merit of these springs long

● ● ●

ago back when both they and the bed were young and could keep secrets.

The sunshine finally returned midmorning as they were stowing away smaller items into boxes that they would ship to the bar in Breckenridge. The larger items like Gabby's mannequin, guitar, and paintings would require special care. Rory was upstairs in Gabby's room as Holden stacked paintings to be shipped when he saw a flash of someone approaching their door. The figure rapped lightly, aware of Holden's eyes upon the window. Holden opened the door to find Madison with her toddler son affixed to her leg. She smiled cordially at Holden as she stroked her son's mop of dark, curly hair.

The boy looked up at Holden with Madison's clear blue eyes and grinned, swiftly putting his chubby thumb in his mouth. Oddly, Holden didn't feel as defensive when Madison was armed with a child. He branded her more

• • •

approachable and human now that her life wasn't attached to Rory's brother.

"Hello, Holden. It's good to see you here." Madison grinned impishly out of the corner of her long full lips. She could see the sweat glistening on Holden's temple that had magically materialized with her presence. The boy reached out his hand to Holden to shake very cordially and adult.

"I'm proud to pump your paw, partner." Holden shook his small, slobbery hand as he jabbered back the phrase to Holden in his own slang.

"Rory has a doctor's appointment at two this afternoon. I was supposed to take her..." Madison paused leaving the sentence leading and open ended.

"Thanks, Madison, I got it." Madison's son opened his arms and reached up to Holden waving his long fingers. Holden picked him up

• • •

and put him on his shoulders, parading around the taped up boxes.

Rory heard voices and poked her head around the door of Gabby's loft catching a glimpse of Holden stomping and bobbing the boy up and down until his giggles got the best of him. Rory stepped into their view and everyone smirked in unison.

"Madison came by about your doctor's appointment today, but I'll take you." Holden returned the boy to his mother's care. Theirs was an odd silence that spoke a thousand words.

"Thank you, Madison." Rory waved from the staircase and Madison saluted her with a wink. Rory disappeared back into the attic.

"For what it's worth, thanks for taking care of Rory." Holden swallowed the lump of pride that had sullied his mood when around Madison. Madison ushered her son to the door.

* * *

"She was my family…now she's yours." Madison shook Holden's hand, passing the appointment card into his palm. She patted it as if it were her son's curly locks. As Madison's navy eyes disappeared behind the door, Holden felt a shift in the balance, relief and release.

The Good Neighbor

She had charm and organized energy

Yet he still sent her packing

Drawn to and yet frustrated

In the things he might be lacking.

Their weeds are much taller

Than the grass they seldom mow

Their children run barefoot

Paying debts they still owe.

His pensive cooperation

Hides his channeled rage

She demands with regret

He decorates his gilded cage.

He wears indiscretions with pride

● ● ●

Merited by kindness

Her insecurities polish each trophy That

perpetuates her blindness.

We all close the blinds at times

As neighbors mop messy floors

The good neighbor hides her eyes. Compassion opens her doors.

Holden closed the front blinds to the beach house that now resembled a skeleton; the couches and beds centered the rooms. It had taken Holden and Rory a week to pack up the house. The boxes taped and labeled for shipping to Breckenridge were stacked by the backdoor. They had been scurrying around from corner to corner; starved rats looking for the minutest crumbs, not wanting to leave any "what if's" or "could have's". They met in the middle of the room. Holden took Rory's hand, threading his long fingers through her petite, slender ones, swinging his arm back and forth, a slow pendulum.

• • •

"This is it." Holden smiled at Rory as she rubbed her belly in circles, proud of the progress report on the pregnancy the doctor had given them.

"No turning back now...looks like you're stuck with me...no more cavorting with that redhead back at the bar." Rory narrowed her eyes, wrinkling her nose in jealous woman fashion.

"Will likes redheads, too. Problem solved. " Rory haughtily poked him in the stomach with her index finger.

"Not my William...He's just a baby!" Rory put her hands on her hips defensively.

"No, *that's* just a baby." Holden poked her stomach with his index finger.

Rory chuckled. Holden scratched his whiskery chin and Rory admired his newfound pride.

"Madison will take care of the rest for us." Rory patted the boxes one last time before Holden

* * *

locked the door. He pried the key in their hiding place, a rotted crevice of an old steel lantern that hung as the outdoor light. Their footsteps rapped in mismatched unison with their lover's chatter, mixed with giggles and growled manly overtones, their jesting silenced with the slam of the car door.

The Good Neighbor

Madison watched their taillights fade into the dawn as she walked the beach toward their freshly vacated house. She sat on their boardwalk steps, pulling her phone from her pocket dialing. A half-lucid voice answered with a questioning hello.

"I don't know where you are or what you are doing, but you need to know that your mission has been accomplished." Madison was firm and direct, biting her lower lip.

* * *

"They reconciled?" Gabby's voice was pitchy from sleep.

"They closed up the house and just left to live in Breckenridge and raise the baby." Madison held her breath, praying Gabby would take the hope and run.

"Closed up…what do you mean?" There was mild panic in Gabby's inflection.

"Rory cleaned the house up. Together, they boxed up everything, particularly your things they wanted to keep. They are being shipped to them in Breckenridge." Gabby's anxiety was palpable through the phone, her huffs measured.

"I didn't think it would hurt so much…to just be a pariah…only a memory." Gabby's voice was a metered murmur.

"You are technically, for all intents and purposes, dead." Madison spoke demonstratively, her tone rehearsed as if for the pulpit crowd.

• • •

"Dead is overrated. I miss the living." Gabby's sarcasm bordered cryptic.

"Sometimes, you have to leave the past where it lies and make new." Madison feared Gabby's yearning.

"I'm a gypsy. Yet, the only place I want to go now is home." Gabby began arguing with her helplessness.

"Give it time, Gabby. This is all so fragile." Madison corralled Gabby's craving with promise. Rhett had always said Gabby wouldn't stay away from Rory and Holden forever.

"You're not my protector anymore, but you are definitely theirs." Gabby's sharp tongue was petulant and goading.

"*You* burned that bridge, Gabby. What makes you think you can walk on water?" Madison challenged Gabby's will.

• • •

"THEY ARE MY FAMILY!" Gabby hurled her misplaced anger and hurt at Madison.

"If you love them, you'll put *them* first, not your regret." Madison caught Gabby's rage softly and with fortitude.

"Regret is powerful motivation. However, our regrets are apples and oranges. Powerful indeed, but they are very singular beasts. " Gabby had only known Madison as Rhett's very loyal spouse. Gabby's own imprisoned life had blinded her to Madison's struggles with this man she idolized as her savior.

"A beast is a beast." Madison wiped away tears her voice masterfully hid.

* * *

• • •

March 2011

Her Eyes

Her eyes hang in her sockets, so aloof

A mini art gallery

Conjectures construed for proof.

Her taut fingers comb the sand, so beige

Snatching for that perfect shell She

childishly blinds age.

Her feet stand certainly, so adept

Besting her monstrosities

Oxymoronic goes each step.

Her smile draws cheeks, so free A

place where macabre devotions

Meet conduit beauty.

Her fertile opinions, so blasé

They chime beyond her sockets Harmonize

her shades of gray.

● ● ●

For Sale

The beach house looked strange with a for sale sign in the yard. It didn't jive with the sand and waves. Even the realtor found the sign didn't sit right in the sand so it had been propped hastily against the porch post. John Vansant had picked the spot, built the house, so it had always had an owner from its inception. It had always had parents, never adopted or abandoned by its family.

Gabby watched the realtor unlock the door with ineptitude. She fought the lock and wrestled rather than finessed the door knob. Her cheesy, almost smarmy announcement of "here it is" covered her disappointment in the odd, empty space. The boards still smelled the same, had distinction like a person's skin. It could be dressed or perfumed, but eventually, the boards had their own scent that transcended time and traffic. It was nostalgic to remember how everything had reeked ... of the beach house when they would return home to Little Rock after a week at the ocean.

With the mere flip of her index finger, Gabby banished the realtor to the porch where she flippantly searched her purse for a cigarette and cell phone. Gabby walked through every room of the house, noting the upgrades that had been made; the fresh paint, the new fixtures, the replacement of carpet. How could they just leave it behind, abandon it so easily? Had it only brought them pain? Could they not remember the joys? Maybe it only represented the ills. She could see that, understood. Gabby was technically gone. Yet, it felt personal and a bit hurtful. As if her existence, her inclusion of them as family hadn't been enough to keep the place.

Gabby strode to the porch to find the realtor, prepared to tell her she wasn't interested in the dilapidated beach house. She reached for the door knob as the door flew open. She jumped backwards a foot before locking eyes with

• • •

William Peacock. Since his parents were selling the house, he had decided to come to the beach house for spring break, never expecting anything but relaxation. He was a beautiful combination of Rory and Holden. Gabby wondered how well he would recognize the dead. Pallor set in and he began to ask questions with his distressful eyes.

"I'm THE Gabby." She extended her spindly fingers in introduction. How did the undead speak?

"You're supposed to be DEAD…" Will's neck flushed like his mother's when faced with anxiety. He stammered as if the synapses in his brain wouldn't fire.

"For all intents and purposes, I am. But, no one is ever really dead unless you forget them, are they?" Gabby retracted her unshaken hand.

"I was trying to decide if I should stay dead when you walked in. Madison warned me to stay dead. I suspect the universe just made

• • •

the decision." Gabby pushed past Will to the door, summoning the realtor to put out her cigarette and come inside.

"I'll take the place for the asking price. Now run along."   The young realtor was flabbergasted, smiling as she closed the door to them.

Gabby could see Will's inexperience in his numb stare. He didn't know how to proceed without losing his composure and control. She remembered that sort of naivety.
It had only punished her with regrets.

"What in the hell just happened?" Will's jaw was clenched, his young body tight with repressed aggressions.

"I bought the house." Gabby began tapping her foot, waiting for the verbal tirade that was soon to follow her smug complacency.

"You ruined our lives…." Will stomped around the room like a pouting toddler. Gabby watched his dramatic display with apathy, rolling her eyes at points.

"I owe *you* nothing, William, my dearest." Gabby's cold frankness incensed Will even more. She could see his misplaced anger and lack of control about the situation channeling toward her.

"Whatever! You're just a...." Will lunged at Gabby, his fists poised to punch through her smugness. Gabby knew he wouldn't strike her. He was too protective of his newfound family to rock the boat. She waited for his initial reaction to quell a bit before responding.

"I accept that I can be a bitch. Honesty feels cruel at times. But, Son, when *you* really hurt one day, you'll find that living is about the little ruinations." Gabby reached around her neck, pulling off a long chain which held a key.

● ● ●

"I just wish you'd stayed dead." Will sighed in frustration, his anger giving in to the reality of the moment.

Will had recognized the necklace. His mother had worn one just like it around her neck when he was just a boy. He had asked Rory about the key. She had told him she and Gabby had found them when they were children. She dangled it in front of Will's grasp.

"I respect your love for them. I can walk away. We can pretend this never happened. It's your choice." Will watched her swing the key in front of him like a hypnotizing pendulum.

"*I* won't tell them I saw you." Will's reason prevailed. "But *you'd* better."

Gabby dropped the key on the ground. Will bent over to snatch it and Gabby stomped on his fingers heartlessly. She had known malice well. It was part of her DNA.

● ● ●

"Save those fists for the bigger evils in your life. They'll serve you well." She pivoted self-righteously before walking away from his threat.

Knock, Knock

The pounding was in multiples of four - hard, angry, and insistent.

It took Madison back to her life with Rhett and the nauseating unpredictability of his associations. She was alone tonight and her cultured instincts served her well.

"Who's there?" She crooned sweetly, loading the clip into her hand gun. Thieves and felons could hear the machinations of steel and bullets through closed doors and would retreat in self-preservation.

"It's Will Peacock. I need to talk to you." Madison lowered the ... gun as she opened the door. Will noticed the polished handgun in her grip. He had never seen her look so serious, her fingers firm on the pistol.

"What is the matter?" Madison noticed the anxiety in his body. His lips were pursed and he was sweating, his shirt collar damp.

"How long have you known Gabby wasn't dead?" Will's eyes met Madison's with scorned interrogation. Madison was the master of disguise. However, there would be no kiting truths today.

Madison offered him a chair, but he paced, running his hand over and over the back of his neck. He had been blindsided and was fighting with trust.

"I came here for spring break...one last party before the beach house sells. I walk in and *she's* there. She just bought the house!" Will sat beside Madison, his eyes tormented, looking for logic.

● ● ●

"I found out after I was married to Rhett. He finally revealed why I had never met Rory. He was hiding and protecting you. She was just another lose end your uncle left me when he died." Madison unloaded the clip from the pistol and set it on the coffee table as she took an insinuating seat.

"After Rhett died, I kept her safe. We don't talk a lot. Shortly after Lexie died, Gabby contacted me when your parents were meeting here. She wanted them to reconcile. When they did and started a new life, I encouraged Gabby to do the same." As Madison spoke, Will put his hands over his face, rubbing at pitchy anger he couldn't wipe away.

"What did she say?" Madison could hear Gabby giving her small sermons of experience, swaying the thirsty.

"She gave me the choice – she offered to walk away..." Will looked at Madison in

● ● ●

bewilderment. Gabby was smooth, gentle with the raw ones.

"But, you didn't let her, did you?" Madison noticed that Will had left his duffle bag outside her door.

"I promised to say nothing. I wanted her to stay dead, yet I threatened her if she didn't reveal herself. If only I hadn't come..." Will threw his head back against the couch. Madison put her hand on his shoulder.

"William, you need to comprehend that you can't control life. You just make choices. She was going to find you all eventually. If nothing more than to prove she mattered, gain a little redemption. Is that so bad? She saved your parents from certain death...she saved you. She had no control, just choices." Will was very far away inside himself, harnessing a swell of feelings that were hopelessly leaking.

* * *

"I just wanted to punch her… evil bitch. My parents will kill her *again*." Will grinned slightly through his scowl.

"Gabby feels uncomfortable mostly because her wisdom is blatant, but always correct. She's suffered more than she'd ever admit. Just look at her paintings. She'll rectify this, trust me." Will stared Gabby's abstract painting hanging on Madison's wall. It entranced him with eccentric logic, made him curious.

"She'd better, Madison. If not, I will make her pay." Will's threat wasn't idle.

Madison opened the front door and snatched his duffle bag, throwing it into his strong hands. She knew he wouldn't stay a night in that house alone with Gabby lurking.

● ● ●

Breckenridge

Holden had been moving boxed up things out of the extra room that was now a freshly painted baby room. It was another spring break happy hour and Rory was manning the bar while he slowly organized and moved his shallow former life into the storage shed. He loved the way she handled the young adults. She was protective and mothering all the while pouring them drinks. Holden heard his cell phone ringing on the kitchen table as he ascended the stairs to their condo.

"Hello, Will." Holden huffed, his lungs taxed.

"Hey, you busy?" Will paced Madison's porch, speaking in a hushed whisper.

"I'm just moving things out of the condo into storage." Holden wondered why he was

. . .

calling during spring break at peak happy hour.

"You guys still coming at the end of the week?" Will's mind postulated ways Gabby would reveal herself.

"Sure, unless you don't want us there?" Holden had entertained the possibility Will had a woman on the sly.

"Oh, no...I just wanted you to know I am staying with Madison. There was a lot of traffic with the realtor...I think she had an offer on the house." Will clenched his fists, trying to even his tenor.

"I guess we should come for sure. This could be the last time." Holden examined his redo on the old bachelor pad. It was now fit for a family.

"How's Mom?" Will secretly prayed she would go into labor before they left.

● ● ●

"She's a hormone waddling around serving spring breakers happy hour and cheese fries." Holden heard the low roar of the crowd in swells of banter.

"Tell her I love her…I'm sorry…" He hated lying to his mother, but especially about Gabby.

"Sorry for what?" Holden felt the hair on the back of his neck crawl slightly.

"Bailing on her…" Will had always taken care of his mother.

"You just have some fun. You never know what kind of woman you might run into on spring break." Holden remembered the bikiniclad women of his youth.

"Yeah." Will grunted a man code sigh Holden feared slightly.

Holden laid his cell phone back on the kitchen counter when it rang again immediately. The area code was Alabama. He answered and

● ● ●

the young realtor was looking for confirmation that it was indeed Mr. Hitchfield speaking. The beach house had a buyer and a sale was pending within the near future she chirped too sweetly, her young, southern voice almost baby talk, casting her as ingenious. Holden thanked the young lady and he told her he would stop by next week when in town. He tossed the phone on the table again.

Holden paused before he picked up a box he thought belonged to Rory. It was an old box with fresh new tape. It had water damage in places, the black markings now faded and gray, the old existing tape yellow and brittle. *Crap* was written hastily on the side. The box had a recent shipping label on it, was sent from the beach house like all the other boxes Madison was now sending to them since they were selling the place. The delivery driver had set it outside the door and it had blended with all the other boxes. He pulled out his pocketknife, cutting the fresh new tape.

* * *

Holden studied the contents of the small box with suspicion, his nose furled.

Inside was an empty bottle of 1990 port wine. For an instant he entertained the idea of Gabby's special code. That only thoroughly incensed Holden's reason. He tossed it aside to add to the shelf that now sported Gabby's empty port wine bottle collection. It was just more of Gabby's crap.

Gabrielle Vansant 2011

"All of us have a little ditty playing in our soul. It will matter to someone that we sing it"

"Art isn't about making things pretty – it's about honesty and that is beautiful."

"One day I'll choose to see the world for what it is...nah."

● ● ●

"Sometimes we forget to see the other car coming at those fated intersections because we are trying to beat the light."

Gabby poured the last glass of chardonnay from the blunt bottle design that had drawn her to purchase it in the first place. The wine labeling was direct, housed in a clear bottle with a black label. The lettering was white and cursive spelling out the word *Bitch* beautifully as if it were straight from Hollywood. Yet it wasn't a *bitch* to open, even had a twist top lid. It was a dry but expensive chardonnay, almost *bitch*slapping the drinker. It had been named appropriately and Gabby knew she would never buy this particular wine again. It was probably going to be a *bitch* to get out of bed after draining the bottle. She deduced it was the perfect bottle to announce her new undead status - facebook old school-style.

Gabby had claimed her roost, drinking in the upstairs window seat of her home. One stark light bulb lit the empty space. It hung in

• • •

the middle of the room from the ceiling by a long electrical cord. Gabby had painted the chord black years ago. It made the white bulb and casing stand out in a skeletal fashion. She had conveniently forgotten to return the key to the obtuse girl at the realtor's office, had kindly promised to return it the next day. So technically, Gabby hadn't broken into the property. She was after all buying the joint.

Gabby watched the old light flicker and pop, vaulting shadows off the walls. Dusk seemed to bring out old demons that gathered like moths to a flame around the solitary light. She could feel the energy of her parents around her, pulling at her appendages in opposite directions, filling her with doubt as their love had all her life. She closed her eyes, meshing with the swish of the waves, quieting those needy, negative undertows. She slipped into her own skin and bones. Bones weary from disease, skin textured and creased in a telling manner reminiscent of the odd moods and colors

• • •

Gabby worked into her canvas. Divine inspiration she had never understood but reverently applied.

Pain and disease had always been a constant in her existence. She quickly deduced that nothing in life was fair or guaranteed. A prosthetic she adapted, learning to coexist with a gracefulness that made MS beautiful; humanity that made it real. She struggled and she saw it as just part of the climb. She didn't cover her disease with denial, but rather a brash honesty that exiled her from typical social norms. For you wouldn't see Gabby coddling the whiniest kid or pandering for acceptance. She wouldn't be found in relationships that were shallow or self-serving. She wanted nothing from no one if they couldn't give her their truths. Gabby had a searing sense of self. Her existence was about sharing her rites.

Gabby stood in the doorway of her room, sponging the vibes around her. The stark light behind her personified her willowy, hourglass shadow. She envisioned two scenarios at the

• • •

homecoming. One involved tears and the other bloodshed. She fisted the heavens, punching specifically at her psychotic father. That had been Gabby's golden noose – fear. John had inadvertently taught her about fear and control. Specifically, the more he feared, the more control he tried to take, the less he truly had. John had loved her just long and purposefully enough as a parent that Gabby had eventually forgiven his neurosis. She hated him for his betrayal of her trust. But, she finally embraced the lessons that made her edges a bit jagged. Gabby was willing to try again. They would hate her, granted. They would shun her. But, she'd loved them long enough and with more purpose that maybe *they'd* forgive her. That is the way Gabby loved; this was their collective home.

Curiosities

Keys inserted into locks are undetectable to most human ears . . . unless the ears have adapted to the sound. Gabby froze in the doorway of her bedroom as she listened to the rather graceless machinations of the intruder. Surely it wasn't the inept realtor girl again? The hands knew the knob enough that nightfall and sneaking weren't foreign to them. The lock finally released but the identity wasn't precisely clear. The smell of alcohol wafted in before the figure stepped through the threshold. Gabby crossed her arms, leaning into the door frame, the harsh light bulb giving her a rock star prowess.

"I hope you aren't going to school to be a gynecologist with those clumsy
        fingers."
Gabby's sarcasm ricocheted off the overpowering smell of cheap booze.

"Do you haunt this place?" Will slurred his words, raising his arms to the sky in frustration.

* * *

"You're a little drunk... interesting." Gabby turned back into her room, ignoring him. Her spastic legs limped to the window seat.

Will's lumbered steps rattled the integrity of the old staircase. He stared at the solitary light bulb in the center of the room, illuminating strange hues his eyes considered psychedelic.

"Why are you here? What do you *really* want from us?" Will's cheeks flushed. He was a bad, inexperienced drinker.

"I can tell your uncle taught you a lot about being an asshole. However, the real question is what are *you* doing here, William? What do *you* want from me?" Gabby turned up the last swig of her wine. He stood swaying back and forth, breathing drunken metered breaths.

"It's my twenty-first birthday today... My friends came down here for spring break to party...we've partied...but... all I could think

● ● ●

about was what you were about to do…why now?" Will's bully turned whiny.

"So you came to judge me and throw a pity party on your birthday for your scorned life? Please, you haven't lived long enough to warrant either." Gabby's hand and leg shook with a slight tremor as she learnedly placed her glass on the window seat. Will noticed Gabby struggling. He remembered her disease. He regrouped his bizarre, buzzed attack.

"I'm sorry if I came off as a jerk…I'm not judging you." He fell to his knees, steadying the uneven world he was viewing, the light bulb changing the colors in the room.

"My mother told me to clean up my mess regarding your parents... Mother's have a beautiful way of manipulating their children, don't you think?" Gabby was nothing like the stories his mother had told him as a child. She was an anomaly.

● ● ●

"Lexie contacted me before she died. I met with her. I helped her put my parents back together." Will watched Gabby's callousness toward his bullish youth retreat a bit.

"So, you've got a little salt and pepper about you. I'll give you that." Will watched the fine lines around Gabby's eyes wink when she talked, telling their own story.

"What happened that night...the night you died?" Gabby knew that Rory had told him nothing for their protection.

"Ah, the truth is on the table now. You got a bit drunk to ask the hard questions, get a leg up on your parents' knowledge…cushion the blow." Gabby joined Will on the floor.

"Whatever…I just need to know *your* side of the story." Will stood back up as Gabby stretched out her aching spastic legs.

● ● ●

"Mine IS the story. There aren't sides. Your parents know very little as intended. They think my father went crazy and I was the fatality. That he was just a fugitive on the run."

"But what was he, really?" Will's buzz was giving in to adrenaline.

"I had a brilliant, chemist for a father who was developing new drug treatments. He was very popular at the time except for the fact that he was crazy and had a penchant for using me all my life as his guinea pig. When I found out I had MS, obviously I hid it from him as long as possible – one more reason I was expendable." The light bulb popped and cracked in bursts of blue and silver flashes.

"My parents didn't know he abused you, did they? That is why you brought them on vacation with you all those years, to shield yourself." Will was wise and perceptive, reading between what was inked on the paper.

● ● ●

"Abuse is such an incorrect description. When it is all you know, you believe, cooperate. It was only after knowing Rory and Holden for years that I realized the testing for what it was. It was a sickness. Knowing them saved my life." Gabby watched the light bounce and buzz – the spirits were restless.

"My parents were *always* in danger, even when you were children? You just never told them." Will had begun to see Gabby's dependence on Holden and Rory for survival.

"I didn't understand when we were children. When I found out I had MS, I began to see that they were in danger by association. I began to plan my escape. My death meant their freedom. I truly didn't know Rory and Holden would sneak off to the boat that night. They hid their relationship from me. Your parents just had rotten timing." The wine made gabby's pain bleed curiously into the blue light.

• • •

"You were screwed either way. That is why my uncle was able to help you. Rhett had everything to gain." Will stood, pacing the creaky wooden floor.

"Rhett knew everything. That last night was staged. I let my father think I had stolen his final papers to his death drug and I ran to the boat as he chased me. He would see me "fall in and drown". I wanted my father to see me die. I wanted the police to never find my body and always make my paranoid father wonder if I was out there with his precious information. I never intended to tangle your parents in this mess. But it is what it is, so I made sure the final piece of damning research never left this house. It will never hurt anyone else." Gabby sat with her legs crossed Indian-style.

"So, you really came back for the final piece of evidence, but ran into me instead?"

● ● ●

Will's logic and deduction were precise. His experience in all things Gabby was not.

"That's so James Bond of you, Will. But my return has little to do with retrieving death drug formulas. What I'm doing doesn't come with reasons I can share with anyone. " Gabby joined Will's ocean view. They stared at one another for an eternal second.

"You mean you won't share them with me." Gabby shoved Will aside, taking back her window seat and ocean view.

"I'm jaded and selfish. Reason enough." Gabby wore self-deprecation like a three karat diamond.

Will attempted to peer behind Gabby's impenetrable eyes and impish upturned grin, but she had the blinds down, no wheels could be seen turning. But he knew they were spinning.

● ● ●

They stood by the window seat, staring out at the flat, seemingly harmless ocean waves that had once drowned their family.

• • •

Revelations

Will prepared the beach house again for Rory and Holden's arrival. They had left beds and couches, the simple necessities that were easily packed when they sold. He checked Gabby's room, making sure there was not even a crumb that would identify she had been there.

Will was to "live his life." That is what Gabby had instructed him to do rather than worry about when or if she would resurface. That was difficult deception for Will, but he found Gabby's plight convincing and surprisingly nonthreatening. Maybe she wasn't all evil? Will had always felt that his mother sensed Gabby on deep, intuitive levels. Maybe he had, too? Madison explained to Will that she thought the two women were so intricately connected, in tune, that there was no plausible way Gabby couldn't reveal herself to Rory.

● ● ●

Old fears had crept up often the last six months. Holden and Rory lived far from story book lives, their relationship tested with the move. Their devotion had allowed them to accept their pasts. Yet, they couldn't deny that they were both scarred from the past twenty years of constantly looking over their shoulders and it bled into their everyday just as it had when they were apart. Their shared silences, their unique coping mechanisms only pacified the unanswered. Holden had scheduled the sale the following day. He wanted this time to finalize the past with the baby coming. He would take charge this time even though doubt hungrily lurked.

Holden and Rory noticed the sold sticker pasted across the *for sale* sign that lay against the patio railing. Rory almost waddled, toting a bag in either arm, the baby testing her equilibrium, her mood sour with exhaustion. Holden felt the pit of his stomach twinge in deep places he hadn't experienced since Rhett had exiled him from

● ● ●

Rory's life. It was as if Holden were waiting for something, anything to change or explain his banishment. He opened the door for her, noticing how nicely Will had tidied the place for them, almost too nicely.

Rory walked into the house, pausing, her eyes instinctively tracking to Gabby's room. She continued walking to the couch before commanding its comfort with a heavy sigh. Holden made several trips to the car, hearing thunder far in the distance. He analyzed the odd distance in Rory's gaze that grew further with each trip to the car. Rory was feeling the dread that had seized him. She was falling into that safe place reserved for the painfully uncomfortable cliffs she often navigated in her life. The air in the beach house felt sticky with a stagnant, shackling energy. It weighted their shoulders and feet with apathy. He yearned to join her safety. He sat on the sofa, rubbing her swollen ankles that now rested in his lap. They smiled slightly at one

* * *

another, comforting their paranoia. It ritually acknowledged their shared fear. Their intuition knew there was a lot more than just a baby on the way.

"You want to make out?" Holden pushed her fat feet aside and moved directly beside her, puckering his full lips.

"You aren't kidding, are you?" Rory found herself forgetting the aura in the room. She was now focused on her body that was an utter mess. Things had shifted places that weren't attractive.

"Nope." He was pulling her into him, into their shared safety and he could feel it working. Holden kissed Rory softly on the side of her mouth, moving his lips wider until she reciprocated. They kissed with their eyes open, calming the other's anxieties, talking with their tongues, getting closer and closer, building

* * *

defenses to their inner ghouls that seemed to revel with each visit to the beach house.

"I truly think this place is inhabited with our bad karma…" Holden started to run his hand below her waist to regions he had recently left uncharted when the baby kicked his hand swiftly.

"It's more than that Holden, you know it, can feel it too…bad vibes." Rory moved closer to him.

"Yea, like something is up…." Holden rose up on his long arms, hovering above her, his eyes squinted as he connected mental dots. Rory stared at his crotch.

"Something's up alright." Rory giggled softly.

Holden nibbled the nape of her neck, making her giggles grow into howls of youthful joy. Foreplay that they had once mastered and now reignited with learned ease. The storm rumbled in the ● ● ● distance, promising

wind and rain. The delicate wind chimes began a
frenetic, off-key refrain. It resounded more
adamantly, a pianist who had placed his fingers on
the wrong keys, playing the notes with pained
disbelief.

Bitch

The storm had knocked out the power
most of the night. The spring evening was cool,
but laced with humidity. Rory and Holden had
opened the windows slightly the night before,
welcoming the breezes as the cool front pushed
through. It was a misty rainy morning on the
beach. The fresh smell of unfamiliar blooming
plants mingled with the salt air. They had slept in,
enjoying the warmth of the bed, the rain slowing
their blood. Their appointment with the realtor
wasn't until around lunch.

● ● ●

Holden lie awake, listening to the light tapping of the rain, watching the raindrops on the window ice skate down the glass. He had bets the drop on the right would fall first, but the left bested chance. He likened his life to the raindrops, still cascading, besting unpredictability. The intimate evening with Rory had lightened his heavy soul. He hadn't touched her since she had gotten large. He didn't let her feel this weight, heavy, cumbersome, exhausting at times. He always tried to smile for her, for the baby. But Rory had sensed his loving hesitation. This baby was frightening. She had experience. Holden loved the thought of a child – a chance to do what he hadn't with Will. He was afraid of the baby, almost afraid of Rory all big and hormonal, an intuitive guru. Holden watched her sleep. She had pushed her hair away from her neck that was damp from hormonal sweats. She was lying on her side, snoring lightly. Rory rolled onto her back, her rotund silhouette comical. He

● ● ●

leaned over and kissed her on the mouth. She didn't move. He pinched her nose closed and a freaky smile grew on her face. She opened her deep green eyes, snorting for air while grabbing his fingers.

"You are having my baby." Holden grinned with fatherly delight. Yet, Rory had caught something off in his tone lately that had been more noticeable the closer she got to her due date.

"Holden, are you afraid?" She probed his face as Holden reached for her, but Rory greeneyed him for an answer.

Holden merely smiled. Rory was beautiful to him right now, desirable in an odd, prideful way

These last nights in this house had him paying attention to the ends they were about to tie and cut. The very ends that had brought them into the people they were today. Hope had a way

● ● ●

of floating the strongest pieces of their broken selves to the surface when parts were drowning in sorrowful undercurrents. Parts of Holden regretted selling the beach house. But, it was time to move away from this chapter, letting the baby give them a new commonality.

They had fallen back asleep, waking with only half hour before their closing appointment. Like two balls, they bounced off one another as if shackled together while rushing for the door. Holden zipped Rory's sundress as she shuffled her feet into her sandals. He held her purse in one hand, the car keys in his mouth. He flung the door open, charging the morning and an empty wine bottle as he plunged into the sand face first.

"Damn spring breakers." Holden spit out a mouthful of sand. He cursed a long line of profanities, dusting the sand off his fresh clothes when he noticed Rory picked up the clear bottle. "Holden…" The corner of Rory's mouth fell south, her lips pursed and quivering. She turned

● ● ●

an empty bottle of 2011 wine toward Holden. The wine's name was *Bitch*.

"NO!" Rory slammed the bottle on the deck, shattering it to bits. They both danced away from the shards of broken glass. They looked at the pieces that reflected a prism of colors scattered across the creamy sand. It was announced. It simply waited to be.

"Let's go sell this house." Holden grabbed Rory's hand, her face and neck splotchy red, her fingers trembling. Holden remembered the 1990 bottle of port wine that he had shoved deep in a box back in Breckenridge.

Dr. Brady Vandeven

The young, hopeless realtor was fashionably late. Holden rapped his anxious fingers on the wooden board room table where they would sign the   • • •   final papers on the beach house sale. Rory noticed a man staring at them through the imposing glass door where they waited. He tried to look away at times, but his eyes intruded on their frustration. "That lucky twit," as Rory referred to their ineffectual female realtor, walked through the door. She shook the waiting man's hand and ushered him toward Rory and Holden. The hair on Rory's arms stood on end.

Dr. Brady Vandeven offered Holden his hand, his height almost matching Holden's. He was a few years older than them, had kind eyes he hid behind thick, black-framed glasses. The realtor went through the standard motions with a perky, almost annoying charm. All the while Mr. Vandeven's eyes bounced back and forth between Rory and Holden in an odd, inquisitive fashion. He was cerebral and quirky with his coy mannerisms. Holden and Rory signed their names, the final line left for the doctor. As the doctor glanced over the papers, his cell phone

● ● ●

vibrated the entire table top. The caller was identified by the name LOWE in all caps. Dr. Vandeven noted the call with a smirk, commenting that it was his twenty-year-old daughter. He had bought the beach house for them to try to spend more time together and mend some old fences. The doctor signed his name, a leftie with a bachelor bare ring finger, smooth hands and fluid fingers accustomed to turning pages, tapping on keypads, or dialing knobs on microscopes. No signs of physical labor existed on his body. Only the fine wrinkles around his eyes and forehead and the salt and pepper glints in his thick head of short cropped hair alluded to the mental gymnastics and brain games he had exerted most of his life.

After the realtor's job was complete, the doctor asked Rory when their baby was due in a kindly voice that was warm, mellow, his tone fine tuned with intellect. The doctor's face seemed to bore and worm deeper than his simple

• • •

question. Rory put her hand on her stomach, giving him the short version of their story the last twenty years. She was concise with a simple two sentence answer as if spilling life history to a stranger on a train. Dr. Vandeven raised his salt and pepper eyebrows, arching them with a grin. His reactions shed light on his own deductions. Apropos - seemed they were all about new beginnings. Holden promised to move the few remainders out of the beach house when they left at the end of the following week. As Rory passed the keys to the house Dr. Vandeven, she felt relief in the doctor's pleasantries as if handing him their past and simply walking away.

Will bounced a faded blue racquetball off the walls of the almost vacant house. The floors echoed the emptiness with a strange reverberation. Will had cleaned up the wine bottle he found shattered on the front porch. He had assumed it was spring break partiers until he saw the label of the bottle. He had remembered

• • •

Gabby drinking the BITCH wine the night they talked in her room. Why would it be shattered on the porch? Will even began to wonder if it had all been an illusion, if time had somehow folded into the past and blended their lives on a parallel unimaginable as seen in movies. Time was a strange bedfellow. Gabby was everywhere and nowhere all at the same time.

His racquetball strayed, bouncing erratically off of boxes and in and out of corners before rolling into the front door where his parents were just returning from signing the closing papers. Holden kicked the ball back at him. They were smiling at Will but he was obviously frowning because their smiles began to mimic his concern. Will fumbled and tripped, chasing the ball, putting concern in his front pocket. He eyed the sale papers in his mother's hand. She flung her purse and the papers on the bar, waddling to the bathroom. Holden's phone chimed and he ducked in the bedroom behind

● ● ●

Rory to answer, closing the door. Will analyzed the papers. Gabrielle Vansant had not bought the house. Maybe she really was a ghost haunting them all.

Goodbye Ghost

Ghosts don't own keys. They unlock the senses of the living. They cause hair on the neck to bristle, drop hearts to the feet while intuitively stirring thoughts of their former selves. They skate through sub consciousness with intention and motive, never to be forsaken. Their resounding impact is seen only in the memories of lessons learned through shared experiences. They haunt like a bat in the belfry.

Gabby had mastered the art of illusion. She worked through the finest cracks or seams undetected. No one heard her roll the deadbolt.

* * *

No one's breathing lapsed as she crept in on the unaware. Her diseased feet were lithe as she tiptoed with a learned precision; MS challenged her to tweak weakness into channeled strengths. Like a mist, she spread her gravity quietly through the room where Rory and Holden slept. She watched their aged baby faces as they snored, ever the children she revered as siblings. Finally, the lovers she had prophesied and praised. The bottle sat on the nightstand by the window, lit by the crescent moon, just inches from Rory's breaths. Gabby's freedom within her achy, numbed fingertips. She held her breath and slid it off the table with a slight bobble. Gabby remembered how Rory was capable of hearing crickets crawl. Apparently the pregnant snores had compromised that gift. Rory sawed logs with the best lumberjacks. As a mist dissipates subtly almost unnoticed, Gabby vanished upstairs. It was the faint hint of her

* * *

skin that was detectable to Rory's heightened nose.

Sleepwalking can be spontaneous if there is an aim. Rory followed her nose, her vision bleary in the darkness, her nose keen. Rory had followed Gabby in the blackest nights. They followed many childhood adventures in this often dark house, lead only by Gabby's scent. An inherent chemistry recognized acutely by lovers or best friends. She tottered up the stairs to Gabby's room, noticing a blue, hazy light coming from under the door. Rory pushed the door open instinctually, not fully comprehending what lay behind it. Gabby sat in the middle of the floor, her legs crossed, her head bowed as if praying or meditating. The blue gray tones of the room contorted Gabby's body into an apparition-like creature, almost ephemeral.

"Are you a ghost?" Rory pleaded in a whiny trance, half asleep and half awake. She

* * *

was sleepwalking, pulled by Gabby's strong connection to her.

"Ghosts don't age, Rory." Gabby looked up at Rory and it was then that the two women were eye to eye for the first time in twenty years.

"How are you alive...Where have you been?" Rory rubbed her eyes, refocusing on Gabby in the odd blue light in the room. Rory walked over to Gabby, her hands shaking violently. She touched Gabby's hair, seeing her aged face.

"I never died...I just escaped." Gabby waited for the full scope of her answer to register through Rory's surprise.

"I don't understand...you escaped and just *left* us?" Rory rubbed her stomach in circular motions, soothing the baby inside that wormed with her shock, giving her sharp pains.

"I never left you. I *protected* you all from things inconceivable. I never meant for you two to

* * *

get involved." Gabby's logic fell on unmoved ears.

"Why should I have to listen to you *now*? Why did you come back after so much lost time?" Rory's voice boomed louder and louder.

"I didn't want to come back. I just wanted to fix you and Holden and leave. But, William found me." Rory winced at the mention of her son's name on Gabby's tongue.

"Don't blame William. How is any of this fair or fixed? Holden and I gave up *everything*." Rory put her hands over her face, sobbing long tears of retribution. Gabby stood, wrapping her arms around Rory as she wept.

"My death was supposed to be your freedom, too. You know you two shouldn't have been on that boat that night. Take a little credit and stop blaming me for *everything*." Rory brashly pushed Gabby and she very quickly lost her compromised balance.

● ● ●

Gabby's MS was now real and very much
a detectable, cruel demon.   She fell to the floor,
struggling to move and get up. The bottle that
held the note she had just thieved from
Rory's nightstand moments earlier shattered into
pieces.

"My Mother wanted me to *explain,* but
my reasons are mine, not for you to understand."
Gabby stared at the shattered bottle, the letter
rolled on the floor mocking her lack of control.

"You are right, Gabby. I don't
understand at all…That's why you have to
remain dead to me…" Rory shredded the note
into a thousand tiny pieces and threw it into the
air. It fell like confetti peppering the floor.
Gabby could feel Rory's seething sadness.

Gabby stared up at Rory in the bluish
light that tinted their tears, cool and distant as
their exiled lives. In that moment of
vulnerability, the past became merely history.

● ● ●

The two thrust fully into the present, no longer petulant children, but adults with scars and lessons. Doors closed that had been left swinging open far too long.

Gabby watched the red flush Rory's neck. Combined with the blue light, it lent a purple tone. Rory moaned a low, growling cry that heightened in pitch, a dog baying at the moon. Her water broke all over the wooden floorboards. Her agonizing cries woke Holden with alarm. He fumbled in the darkness for his glasses. His long legs scaled the stairs to the sound of Rory's wails. Holden stood in the doorway, wondering if he had entered a time portal. The purplish, blue light gave the two women unclear features, blobs of spirit energy, writhing and contorting. Holden knew the woman cradling Rory with fervency and regret was no ghost. He moved toward them, putting a hand on Gabby's shoulder, the tender man, always Gabby's brother. He didn't question, just placed the

* * *

puzzle pieces appropriately. Holden's fingers squeezed Gabby's shoulder with firm understanding, just as firm as Rory's quaked with fury and disdain.

The trio was an odd family, yet family no matter how they denied it. Their goal now was to work together. It would be their final swan song. The baby was crowning fast. Gabby moved between Rory's legs. Holden supported Rory's torso and head. Gabby assumed her role as the bossy diva. Rory screamed and suffered through the pain with dignity. Holden shored up the trio. Roles and genetics they had played their whole lives whether together or apart.

Will stood in the doorway, his mother and father's backs to him as Gabby's voodoo eyes worked magic. He observed first-hand the dynamic of the people who had created him. Minutes felt like hours as Rory struggled and Gabby manipulated and controlled the birth.

* * *

Gabby's hands were contorted and messy, blood and bodily fluids her medium. The baby acted as Gabby's paint brush, the floor with broken glass and shards of paper now her canvas. Rory screamed in the longest, most agonizing vocals. Gabby manipulated and gave breath to the most beautiful art she would ever produce.

Tiny yelps from new lungs ricocheted off the attic room's high ceiling, giving the cries an angelic quality. Rory grew silent. She had lost a lot of blood and was weak and exhausted. Gabby held up a tiny, red blob, cutting the umbilical cord, deeming it a girl before handing her to Rory. Gabby knew they'd never be in the same room together again like this. The dynamic had now shifted. The karma filled air was charged with unspoken love and goodbyes, spirit seeds.

"Her name is Hope." Rory whispered, kissing the baby girl on her dirty, bald head.

● ● ●

"Will and Hope. Strong words to live by." Will joined their jaded reunion from the doorway after calling 911. He and Gabby shared a slight smile.

Just Like That

Gabby mimicked the night becoming the darkness once again. She tidied up the upstairs room, wiping her canvas clean. Just like that the scene was now only a memory. The ambulance had arrived and the EMT's had talked with Gabby briefly before taking a very weary Rory and baby. Holden followed the ambulance. Rory vividly remembered the EMT's gossiping openly about the lady who delivered baby Hope. They referred to Gabby as a witchy woman with "mad skills."

The unexpected birth had delayed Holden and Rory's moving and departure from the beach

* * *

house almost a week. Today was moving day. Will had been instrumental in organizing the

final furniture and boxes for the move, missing a week from college to help his parents start over in Breckenridge, far away from *this* beach. A new round of spring breakers had arrived to party. Will watched them drink and dance, feeling so isolated and different from them, weighted with his vast and bizarre life experience. Will thought about Gabby often, wondering about the secrets that she shared surrounding her death and the ones she wouldn't share with him. Baby Hope was a joyful baby with an easy temperament, her smiles filling in the unspoken regarding her birth. He thought of how his baby sister cooed and wiggled in her crib and he was determined Hope would be like that spring break crowd – joyful and carefree without the weight of the world.

Holden and Rory were taking a flight out of Mobile. They packed their luggage into the car

• • •

and drove away uneventfully. Holden elbowed Rory referencing a young redheaded gal walking the beach moving toward the beach house. Rory smirked at him. She stroked Hope's bald head, praying there were no signs of red peach fuzz.

Traffic had been intense most of the morning with teenagers moving back and forth across the sand. Will had loaded the last boxes into the moving van he was driving back to their home in Breckenridge. He was casing the house one last time and didn't notice the figure standing at the front door until he heard a key jiggle in the unlocked knob. In walked a red headed girl with cut-off shorts and a tank top.

"Oh, I'm so sorry...I didn't realize you were still moving out." The girl seemed overly embarrassed, even startled, her freckles turning crimson to match her hair. She began closing the door poised to disappear.

* * *

"Wait – are you here for spring break?" Will was sure the girl thought he was just a mover. He found himself suspicious because she had a key.

"Not really…I'm sorry for intruding. I can come back later…" Again, the girl postured to leave, yet nosy, taunting him to invite her to stay.

"Wait - I'm almost packed up here. My family should have already moved. Sorry. I assume you know the new owner… you have a key?" Will looked at the shiny silver key she nervously rolled in her left hand. The girl looked around the room and Will watched her porcelain face with fascination.

"Oh, you're not the mover. I'm being so rude…just barging in on you as you try to move out." Her words were sincere and apologetic, yet her actions were desperate and inquisitive.

● ● ●

"I'm guessing Dr. Vandeven is your father?" Will caught her off guard again, her mouth contorting. They exchanged an awkward grin.

"Yes, I'm Lowe Vandeven." She extended her hand in an odd, formal way, their fingers locking longer than the social norm. He could tell she wasn't a spring break party girl at all.

"I'm Will." His stomach swam with curiosity about her motivations. She appeared clumsy and nervous, her eyes all over the house.

"Can I help you find something? Those are all your father's boxes..." Will's presence had foiled something covert. Will watched Lowe eyeball a large specially made box, one reserved for paintings.

"My father doesn't know I am here......" Lowe fidgeted nervously with the frayed hem of her cut-off jean shorts.

* * *

"It's your house now. Take whatever you want. " Will smiled, giving her permission to rifle through her father's things. They shared an odd, familiar ease like partners in crime.

"Actually, I'm looking for my mother." Lowe began opening the specialty box, pulling out paintings until she found the one that seemed to make her so very proud. The painting was abstract signed BRIE Vandeven.

"Your *mother* painted this?" Will's neck flushed purple. The hair on the back of his neck bristled.

"Yes…she is an artist…my parents bought this house so we can reconnect." Lowe dug through boxes, hoping to find any hint of her mother.

"You aren't close with her?" Will interrogated her innocently.

"Oh, yes…very close…see, my mother has been estranged… it's complicated…She's

• • •

been so very sick most of her life. I don't know why I am telling you this." Lowe pushed the boxes aside in frustration, looking around the room once again.

"May I ask why you keep searching an empty room instead of the boxes?" Will's sincerity was inadvertently earning Lowe's trust. She got tears in her big blue eyes as she searched the corners of the rooms.

"It's stupid really…My mother always leaves me little notes… in cute bottles...tucked someplace special…that's our thing." Will reached in his pocket for the key to the upstairs room.

"You might check the attic room upstairs." Will tenderly placed a key in Lowe's skinny fingers. She wiped the tears from her cheek and raced up the unbalanced steps.

Will put his hands in his jean pockets, listening to Lowe scurry around the empty attic

● ● ●

room. She shrieked with a coo of odd exhilaration as she descended the stairs like a gymnast.

"I found it…I knew she wouldn't forget me…she promised…How did you think of the attic?" Lowe held a blown blue glass bottle that had a rolled up piece of paper inside.

"Call it a hunch." They sheepishly stared at one another with an unspoken understanding.

Will helped her fish the note out, their fingertips' touching often sending odd sparks down his spine. He was certain in that second that there were cosmic powers making sure that each person in life bumped into the right energies at just the right time. It was in this chance encounter he became aware that his tremendous life and experience could matter to the right someone else. Fate had taken over, redeeming faith in the human conditions of love and forgiveness.

● ● ●

"My mother, my Gabby, is just the most *amazing* person." Lowe unrolled the note and read it aloud.

Spirit Seeds

Drone or bubbly

Our physicality is fleeting. Riddled with

sagging skin and laugh lines For the

DNA performs its due diligence.

Imperfections

Rile and possess

Artists and poets monopolize

Soften or harden the angst.

Truth is…

Lovely talents, gifts

Magnificence from the most mangled little finger Wilts

doubt, ratifying our tiniest boons.

● ● ●

Glamorous old ladies are made,

Sprouting from the inside out

Aging with vanity of a leathered man That

cultivates golden spirit seeds.

Rotting skin the virtue

For life is to be squeezed,

Every drop of urgent inspiration Used

on the thirstiest and least.

~G.V.

● ● ●

• • •